Contents

Meet **Fred Gipson**

Fred Gipson was born and died in Mason County, Texas, in the same hill country where *Old Yeller* takes place. Like young Arliss, he spent a lot of time in the woods watching animals. He also talked with "old-timers" — people who had lived in Texas for many years. Listening to their tales and those his father told helped Gipson develop his love for storytelling. He said that he especially enjoyed writing stories for young people because all they ask is that the author "write a simple and honest tale."

Old Yeller, Gipson's second book for children, was an instant success when it was published. It was named a Newbery Honor book in 1957 and was made into a popular movie that same year. Gipson wrote the screenplay for the film version of *Old Yeller*.

Old Yeller

FRED GIPSON

HOUGHTON MIFFLIN COMPANY

BOSTON

ATLANTA   DALLAS   GENEVA, ILLINOIS   PALO ALTO   PRINCETON

Acknowledgments

Grateful acknowledgment is made for use of the following material:

Text

1 *Old Yeller,* by Fred Gipson. Copyright © 1956 by Fred Gipson. Reprinted by permission of HarperCollins Publishers. **190** 1879 letter from a Coleman County woman as it appeared in "Day Ranch and Neighboring Ranches," by Col. Jame T. Padgitt, from the *Edwards Plateau Historian,* Volume VI, 1974–1979, pp. 34–36. **194** *Cowboys and Cattle Ranching: Yesterday and Today,* by Patricia Lauber. Copyright © 1973 by Patricia Lauber. Reprinted by permission of the author.

Illustrations

192–193 Leslie Evans.

Photography

ii Clayton Schmidt/courtesy of Harper Collins. **185** Allan D. Cruickshank from National Audubon Society/Photo Researchers (cl); Kunio Owaki/The Stock Market (b). **186** Leonard Lee Rue III/Photo Researchers, Inc. (t); © Art Wolfe/©Tony Stone Images/Chicago Inc. (cl); © Daniel J. Cox/©Tony Stone Images/Chicago Inc. (cr); © Leonard Lee Rue III/© Tony Stone Images/Chicago (bl). **187** © Maslowski Photo/Photo Researchers (tl); © Nell Bolen/Photo Researchers (tr); Leonard Lee Rue III/Photo Researchers, Inc. (cr); Richard T. Bryant (bl, br). **188** Alexander Lowry/Photo Researchers (tl); Leonard Lee Rue III/Photo Researchers, Inc. (tr); © Art Wolfe/©Tony Stone Images/Chicago Inc. (c); © Renee Lynn/©Tony Stone Images/Chicago Inc. (b). **189** Stephen J Krasemannn/DRK Photo (tl); Tom & Pat Leeson/Photo Researchers (tr); Horst Bielfeld from the National Audubon Society/Photo Researchers (c); Leonard Lee Rue III/Photo Researchers, Inc. (br). **190** Mason County Historical Commission. **194** Becky Chambers (cover). **194–195** Library, The State Historical Society of Colorado (c). **195** Kansas State Historical Society, Topeka, Kansas (tr). **196** Erwin E. Smith Collection, Library of Congress (t); The Paul Stewart Collection, Black American West Museum (b). **197** Denver Public Library, Western History Department (t); Erwin E. Smith Collection, Library of Congress (b). **198** Denver Public Library, Western History Department (l). **198–199** Alan J. Kania/The State Historical Society of Colorado (t). **199** Montgomery Ward and Company, 1895 (br). **200** Erwin E. Smith Collection, Library of Congress (t); Leonard Lee Rue III from National Audubon Society/Photo Researchers (b).

1999 Impression
Houghton Mifflin Edition, 1996

ISBN 0-395-73259-X

Old Yeller

ONE

We called him Old Yeller. The name had a sort of double meaning. One part meant that his short hair was a dingy yellow, a color that we called "yeller" in those days. The other meant that when he opened his head, the sound he let out came closer to being a yell than a bark.

I remember like yesterday how he strayed in out of nowhere to our log cabin on Birdsong Creek. He made me so mad at first that I wanted to kill him. Then, later, when I had to kill him, it was like having to shoot some of my own folks. That's how much I'd come to think of the big yeller dog.

1

He came in the late 1860's, the best I remember. Anyhow, it was the year that Papa and a bunch of other Salt Licks settlers formed a "pool herd" of their little separate bunches of steers and trailed them to the new cattle market at Abilene, Kansas.

This was to get "cash money," a thing that all Texans were short of in those years right after the Civil War. We lived then in a new country and a good one. As Papa pointed out the day the men talked over making the drive, we had plenty of grass, wood, and water. We had wild game for the killing, fertile ground for growing bread corn, and the Indians had been put onto reservations with the return of U.S. soldiers to the Texas forts.

"In fact," Papa wound up, "all we lack having a tight tail-holt on the world is a little cash money. And we can get that at Abilene."

Well, the idea sounded good, but some of the men still hesitated. Abilene was better than six hundred miles north of the Texas hill country we lived in. It would take months for the men to make the drive and ride back home. And all that time the womenfolks and children of Salt Licks would be left in a wild frontier settlement to make out the best they could.

Still, they needed money, and they realized that whatever a man does, he's bound to take some risks. So they talked it over with each other and with their women and decided it was the thing to do. They told their folks what to do in case the Indians came off the reservation or the coons got to eating the corn or the bears got to killing too many hogs. Then they gathered their cattle, burned a trail brand on their hips, and pulled out on the long trail to Kansas.

I remember how it was the day Papa left. I remember his standing in front of the cabin with his horse saddled, his gun in his scabbard, and his bedroll tied on back of the cantle. I remember how tall and straight and handsome he looked, with his high-crowned hat and his black mustaches drooping in cow-horn curves past the corners of his mouth. And I remember how Mama was trying to keep from crying because he was leaving and how Little Arliss, who was only five and didn't know much, wasn't trying to keep from crying at all. In fact, he was howling his head off; not because Papa was leaving, but because he couldn't go, too.

I wasn't about to cry. I was fourteen years old, pretty near a grown man. I stood back and didn't let on for a minute that I wanted to cry.

Papa got through loving up Mama and Little Arliss and mounted his horse. I looked up at him. He motioned for me to come along. So I walked beside his horse down the trail that led under the big liveoaks and past the spring.

When he'd gotten out of hearing of the house, Papa reached down and put a hand on my shoulder.

"Now, Travis," he said, "you're getting to be a big boy; and while I'm gone, you'll be the man of the family. I want you to act like one. You take care of Mama and Little Arliss. You look after the work and don't wait around for your mama to point out what needs to be done. Think you can do that?"

"Yessir," I said.

"Now, there's the cows to milk and wood to cut and young pigs to mark and fresh meat to shoot. But mainly there's the corn patch. If you don't work it right or if you let the varmints eat up the roasting ears, we'll be without bread corn for the winter."

"Yessir," I said.

"All right, boy. I'll be seeing you this fall."

4

I stood there and let him ride on. There-wasn't any more to say.

Suddenly I remembered and went running down the trail after him, calling for him to wait.

He pulled up his horse and twisted around in the saddle. "Yeah, boy," he said. "What is it?"

"That horse," I said.

"What horse?" he said, like he'd never heard me mention it before. "You mean you're wanting a horse?"

"Now, Papa," I complained. "You know I've been aching all over for a horse to ride. I've told you time and again."

I looked up to catch him grinning at me and felt foolish that I hadn't realized he was teasing.

"What you're needing worse than a horse is a good dog."

"Yessir," I said, "but a horse is what I'm wanting the worst."

"All right," he said. "You act a man's part while I'm gone, and I'll see that you get a man's horse to ride when I sell the cattle. I think we can shake on that deal."

He reached out his hand, and we shook. It was the first time I'd ever shaken hands like a man. It made me feel big and solemn and important in a way I'd never felt before. I knew then that I could handle whatever needed to be done while Papa was gone.

I turned and started back up the trail toward the cabin. I guessed maybe Papa was right. I guessed I could use a dog. All the other settlers had dogs. They were big fierce cur dogs that the settlers used for catching hogs and driving cattle and fighting coons out of the cornfields. They kept them as watchdogs against the depredations of loafer wolves, bears, panthers, and raiding Indians. There was no question about it: for the sort of country we lived in, a good dog around the place was sometimes worth more than two or three men. I knew this as well as anybody, because the summer before I'd had a good dog.

His name was Bell. He was nearly as old as I was. We'd had him ever since I could remember. He'd protected me from rattlesnakes and bad hogs while I was little. He'd hunted with me when I was bigger. Once he'd dragged me out of Birdsong Creek when I was about to drown and another time he'd given warning in time to keep

6

some raiding Comanches from stealing and eating our mule, Jumper.

Then he'd had to go act a fool and get himself killed.

It was while Papa and I were cutting wild hay in a little patch of prairie back of the house. A big diamond-back rattler struck at Papa and Papa chopped his head off with one quick lick of his scythe. The head dropped to the ground three or four feet away from the writhing body. It lay there, with the ugly mouth opening and shutting, still trying to bite something.

As smart as Bell was, you'd have thought he'd have better sense than to go up and nuzzle that rattler's head. But he didn't, and a second later, he was falling back, howling and slinging his own head till his ears popped. But it was too late then. That snake mouth had snapped shut on his nose, driving the fangs in so deep that it was a full minute before he could sling the bloody head loose.

He died that night, and I cried for a week. Papa tried to make me feel better by promising to get me another dog right away, but I wouldn't have it. It made me mad just to think about some other dog's trying to take Bell's place.

And I still felt the same about it. All I wanted now was a horse.

The trail I followed led along the bank of Birdsong Creek through some bee myrtle bushes. The bushes were blooming white and smelled sweet. In the top of one a mockingbird was singing. That made me recollect how Birdsong Creek had got its name. Mama had named it when she and Papa came to settle. Mama had told me about it. She said she named it the first day she and Papa got there, with Mama driving the ox cart loaded with our house plunder, and with Papa driving the cows and horses. They'd meant to build closer to the other settlers, over on Salt Branch. But they'd camped there at the spring; and the bee myrtle had been blooming white that day, and seemed like in every bush there was a mockingbird, singing his fool head off. It was all so pretty and smelled so good and the singing birds made such fine music that Mama wouldn't go on.

"We'll build right here," she'd told Papa.

And that's what they'd done. Built themselves a home right here on Birdsong Creek and fought off the Indians and cleared a corn patch and raised me and Little Arliss and lost a little sister who died of a fever.

Now it was my home, too. And while Papa was gone, it was up to me to look after it.

I came to our spring that gushed clear cold water out of a split in a rock ledge. The water poured into a pothole about the size of a wagon bed. In the pothole, up to his ears in the water, stood Little Arliss. Right in our drinking water!

I said: "*Arliss!* You get out of that water."

Arliss turned and stuck out his tongue at me.

"I'll cut me a sprout!" I warned.

All he did was stick out his tongue at me again and splash water in my direction.

I got my knife out and cut a green mesquite sprout. I trimmed all the leaves and thorns off, then headed for him.

Arliss saw then that I meant business. He came lunging up out of the pool, knocking water all over his clothes lying on the bank. He lit out for the house, running naked and screaming bloody murder. To listen to him, you'd have thought the Comanches were lifting his scalp.

Mama heard him and came rushing out of the cabin. She saw Little Arliss running naked. She saw me following after him with a mesquite sprout in one hand and his clothes in the other. She called out to me.

"Travis," she said, "what on earth have you done to your little brother?"

I said, "Nothing yet. But if he doesn't keep out of our drinking water, I'm going to wear him to a frazzle."

That's what Papa always told Little Arliss when he caught him in the pool. I figured if I had to take Papa's place, I might as well talk like him.

Mama stared at me for a minute. I thought she was fixing to argue that I was getting too big for my britches. Lots of times she'd tell me that. But this time she didn't. She just smiled suddenly and grabbed Little Arliss by one ear and held on. He went to hollering and jumping up and down and trying to pull away, but she held on till I got there with his clothes. She put them on him and told him: "Look here, young squirrel. You better listen to your big brother Travis if you want to keep out of trouble." Then she made him go sit still awhile in the dog run.

The dog run was an open roofed-over space between the two rooms of our log cabin. It was a good place to eat watermelons in the hot summer or to sleep when the night breezes weren't strong enough to push through the cracks between the cabin logs. Sometimes we hung up fresh-killed meat there to cool out.

Little Arliss sat in the dog run and sulked while I packed water from the spring. I packed the water in a bucket that Papa had made out of the hide of a cow's leg. I poured the water into the ash hopper that stood beside the cabin. That was so the water could trickle down through the wood ashes and become lye water. Later Mama would mix this lye water with hog fat and boil it in an iron pot when she wanted to make soap.

When I went to cut wood for Mama, though, Little Arliss left the dog run to come watch me work. Like always, he stood in exactly the right place for the chips from my axe to fly up and maybe knock his eyeballs out. I said: "You better skin out for that house, you little scamp!" He skinned out, too. Just like I told him. Without even sticking out his tongue at me this time.

And he sat right there till Mama called us to dinner.

After dinner, I didn't wait for Mama to tell me that I needed to finish running out the corn middles. I got right up from the table and went out and hooked Jumper to the double shovel. I started in plowing where Papa had left off the day before. I figured that if I got an early start, I could finish the corn patch by sundown.

Jumper was a dun mule with a narrow black stripe running along his backbone between his mane and tail. Papa had named him Jumper because nobody yet had ever built a fence he couldn't jump over. Papa claimed Jumper could clear the moon if he took a notion to see the other side of it.

Jumper was a pretty good mule, though. He was gentle to ride; you could pack in fresh meat on him; and he was willing about pulling a plow. Only, sometimes when I plowed him and he decided quitting time had come, he'd stop work right then. Maybe we'd be out in the middle of the field when Jumper got the notion that it was time to quit for dinner. Right then, he'd swing around and head for the cabin, dragging down corn with the plow and paying no mind whatever to my hauling back on the reins and hollering "Whoa!"

Late that evening, Jumper tried to pull that stunt on me again; but I was laying for him. With Papa gone, I knew I had to teach Jumper a good lesson. I'd been plowing all afternoon, holding a green cedar club between the plow handles.

I still lacked three or four corn rows being finished when sundown came and Jumper decided it was quitting time. He let out a long bray and started wringing his tail. He left the middle he was traveling in. He struck out through the young corn, headed for the cabin.

I didn't even holler "Whoa!" at him. I just threw the looped reins off my shoulder and ran up beside him. I drew back my green cedar club and whacked him so hard across the jawbone that I nearly dropped him in his tracks.

You never saw a worse surprised mule. He snorted, started to run, then just stood there and stared at me. Like maybe he couldn't believe that I was man enough to club him that hard.

I drew back my club again. "Jumper," I said, "if you don't get back there and finish this plowing job, you're going to get more of the same. You understand?"

I guess he understood, all right. Anyhow, from then on till we were through, he stayed right on the job. The only thing he did different from what he'd have done with Papa was to travel with his head turned sideways, watching me every step of the way.

When finally I got to the house, I found that Mama had done the milking and she and Little Arliss were waiting supper on me. Just like we generally waited for Papa when he came in late.

I crawled into bed with Little Arliss that night, feeling pretty satisfied with myself. Our bed was a corn-shuck mattress laid over a couple of squared-up cowhides that had been laced together. The cowhides stood about two feet off the dirt floor, stretched tight inside a pole frame Papa had built in one corner of the room. I lay there and listened to the corn shucks squeak when I breathed and to the owls hooting in the timber along Birdsong Creek. I guessed I'd made a good start. I'd done my work without having to be told. I'd taught Little Arliss and Jumper that I wasn't to be trifled with. And Mama could already see that I was man enough to wait supper on.

I guessed that I could handle things while Papa was gone just about as good as he could.

TWO

It was the next morning when the big yeller dog came.

I found him at daylight when Mama told me to step out to the dog run and cut down a side of middling meat hanging to the pole rafters.

The minute I opened the door and looked up, I saw that the meat was gone. It had been tied to the rafter with bear-grass blades braided together for string. Now nothing was left hanging to the pole but the frazzled ends of the snapped blades.

I looked down then. At the same instant, a dog rose from where he'd been curled up on the ground beside the barrel that held our cornmeal. He was a big ugly slick-haired yeller dog. One short ear had been chewed clear off and his tail had been bobbed so close to his rump that there was hardly stub enough left to wag. But the most noticeable thing to me about him was how thin and starved looking he was, all but for his belly. His belly was swelled up as tight and round as a pumpkin.

It wasn't hard to tell how come that belly was so full. All I had to do was look at the piece of curled-up rind lying in the dirt beside him, with all the meat gnawed off. That side of meat had been a big one, but now there wasn't enough meat left on the rind to interest a pack rat.

Well, to lose the only meat we had left from last winter's hog butchering was bad enough. But what made me even madder was the way the dog acted. He didn't even have the manners to feel ashamed of what he'd done. He rose to his feet, stretched, yawned, then came romping toward me, wiggling that stub tail and yelling *Yow! Yow! Yow!* Just like he belonged there and I was his best friend.

"Why, you thieving rascal!" I shouted and kicked at him as hard as I could.

16

He ducked, just in time, so that I missed him by a hair. But nobody could have told I missed, after the way he fell over on the ground and lay there, with his belly up and his four feet in the air, squawling and bellering at the top of his voice. From the racket he made, you'd have thought I had a club and was breaking every bone in his body.

Mama came running to stick her head through the door and say, "What on earth, Travis?"

"Why, this old stray dog has come and eaten our middling meat clear up," I said.

I aimed another kick at him. He was quick and rolled out of reach again, just in time, then fell back to the ground and lay there, yelling louder than ever.

Then out came Little Arliss. He was naked, like he always slept in the summer. He was hollering "A dog! A dog!" He ran past me and fell on the dog and petted him till he quit howling, then turned on me, fighting mad.

"You quit kicking my dog!" he yelled fiercely. "You kick my dog, and I'll wear you to a frazzle!"

The battling stick that Mama used to beat the dirt out of clothes when she washed stood leaning against the wall. Now, Little

Arliss grabbed it up in both hands and came at me, swinging.

It was such a surprise move, Little Arliss making fight at me that way, that I just stood there with my mouth open and let him clout me a good one before I thought to move. Then Mama stepped in and took the stick away from him.

Arliss turned on her, ready to fight with his bare fists. Then he decided against it and ran and put his arms around the big dog's neck. He began to yell: "He's my dog. You can't kick him. He's my dog!"

The big dog was back up on his feet now, wagging his stub tail again and licking the tears off Arliss's face with his pink tongue.

Mama laughed. "Well, Travis," she said, "it looks like we've got us a dog."

"But Mama," I said. "You don't mean we'd keep an old ugly dog like that. One that will come in and steal meat right out of the house."

"Well, maybe we can't keep him," Mama said. "Maybe he belongs to somebody around here who'll want him back."

"He doesn't belong to anybody in the settlement," I said. "I know every dog at Salt Licks."

"Well, then," Mama said. "If he's a stray,

there's no reason why Little Arliss can't claim him. And you'll have to admit he's a smart dog. Mighty few dogs have sense enough to figure out a way to reach a side of meat hanging that high. He must have climbed up on top of that meal barrel and jumped from there."

I went over and looked at the wooden lid on top of the meal barrel. Sure enough, in the thin film of dust that had settled over it were dog tracks.

"Well, all right," I admitted. "He's a smart dog. But I still don't want him."

"Now, Travis," Mama said. "You're not being fair. You had you a dog when you were little, but Arliss has never had one. He's too little for you to play with, and he gets lonely."

I didn't say any more. When Mama got her mind set a certain way, there was no use in arguing with her. But I didn't want that meat-thieving dog on the place, and I didn't aim to have him. I might have to put up with him for a day or so, but sooner or later, I'd find a way to get rid of him.

Mama must have guessed what was going on in my mind, for she kept handing me sober looks all the time she was getting breakfast.

She fed us cornmeal mush cooked in a pot swung over the fireplace. She sweetened it with wild honey that Papa and I had cut out of a bee tree last fall, and added cream skimmed off last night's milk. It was good eating; but I'd had my appetite whetted for fried middling meat to go with it.

Mama waited till I was done, then said: "Now, Travis, as soon as you've milked the cows, I think you ought to get your gun and try to kill us a fat young doe for meat. And while you're gone, I want you to do some thinking on what I said about Little Arliss and this stray dog."

THREE

All right, I was willing to go make a try for a fat doe. I was generally more than willing to go hunting. And while I was gone, I might do some thinking about Little Arliss and that thieving stray dog. But I didn't much think my thinking would take the turn Mama wanted.

I went and milked the cows and brought the milk in for Mama to strain. I got my rifle and went out to the lot and caught Jumper. I tied a rope around his neck, half-hitched a noose around his nose and pitched the rest of the rope across his back. This was the rope I'd rein him with. Then I got me a sec-

ond rope and tied it tight around his middle, just back of his withers. This second
rope I'd use to tie my deer onto Jumper's
back—if I got one.

Papa had shown me how to tie a deer's
feet together and pack it home across my
shoulder, and I'd done it. But to carry a
deer very far like that was a sweat-popping
job that I'd rather leave to Jumper. He was
bigger and stronger.

I mounted Jumper bareback and rode
him along Birdsong Creek and across a
rocky hog-back ridge. I thought how fine it
would be if I was riding my own horse instead of an old mule. I rode down a long
sweeping slope where a scattering of huge,
ragged-topped liveoaks stood about in grass
so tall that it dragged against the underside
of Jumper's belly. I rode to within a quarter
of a mile of the Salt Licks, then left Jumper
tied in a thicket and went on afoot.

I couldn't take Jumper close to the Licks
for a couple of reasons. In the first place,
he'd get to swishing his tail and stomping his
feet at flies and maybe scare off my game.
On top of that, he was gun shy. Fire a gun
close to Jumper, and he'd fall to staves. He'd
snort and wheel to run and fall back against
his tie rope, trying to break loose. He'd bawl

and paw the air and take on like he'd been shot. When it came to gunfire Jumper didn't have any more sense than a red ant in a hot skillet.

It was a fine morning for hunting, with the air still and the rising sun shining bright on the tall green grass and the greener leaves of the timber. There wasn't enough breeze blowing for me to tell the wind direction, so I licked one finger and held it up. Sure enough, the side next to me cooled first. That meant that what little push there was to the air was away from me, toward the Salt Licks. Which wouldn't do at all. No deer would come to the Licks if he caught wind of me first.

I half circled the Licks till I had the breeze moving across them toward me and took cover under a wild grapevine that hung low out of the top of a gnarled oak. I sat down with my back against the trunk of the tree. I sat with my legs crossed and my rifle cradled on my knees. Then I made myself get as still as the tree.

Papa had taught me that, 'way back when I was little, the same as he'd taught me to hunt downwind from my game. He always said: "It's not your shape that catches a deer's eye. It's your moving. If a deer can't smell you and can't see you move, he won't ever know you're there."

So I sat there, holding as still as a stump, searching the clearing around the Licks.

The Licks was a scattered outcropping of dark rocks with black streaks in them. The black streaks held the salt that Papa said had got mixed up with the rocks a jillion years ago. I don't know how he knew what had happened so far back, but the salt was there, and all the hogs and cattle and wild animals in that part of the country came there to lick it.

One time, Papa said, when he and Mama had first settled there, they'd run clean out of salt and had to beat up pieces of the rock and boil them in water. Then they'd used the salty water to season their meat and cornbread.

Wild game generally came to lick the rocks in the early mornings or late evenings, and those were the best times to come for meat. The killer animals, like bear and panther and bobcats, knew this and came to the Licks at the same time. Sometimes we'd get a shot at them. I'd killed two bobcats and a wolf there while waiting for deer; and once Papa shot a big panther right after it had leaped on a mule colt and broken its neck with one slap of its heavy forepaw.

I hoped I'd get a shot at a bear or panther this morning. The only thing that showed up, however, was a little band of javelina hogs, and I knew better than to shoot them. Make a bad shot and wound one so that he went to squealing, and you had the whole bunch after you, ready to eat you alive. They were small animals. Their tushes weren't as long as those of the range hogs we had running wild in the woods. They couldn't cut you as deep, but once javelinas got after you, they'd keep after you for a lot longer time.

Once Jed Simpson's boy Rosal shot into a bunch of javelinas and they took after him. They treed him up a mesquite and kept him there from early morning till long after suppertime. The mesquite was a small one, and they nearly chewed the trunk of it in two trying to get to him. After that Rosal was willing to let the javelinas alone.

The javelinas moved away, and I saw some bobwhite quail feed into the opening around the Licks. Then here came three cows with young calves and a roan bull. They stood and licked at the rocks. I watched them awhile, then got to watching a couple of squirrels playing in the top of a tree close to the one I sat under.

The squirrels were running and jumping and chattering and flashing their tails in the sunlight. One would run along a tree branch, then take a flying leap to the next branch. There it would sit, fussing, and wait to see if the second one had the nerve to jump that far. When the second squirrel did, the first one would set up an excited chatter and make a run for a longer leap. Sure enough, after a while, the leader tried to jump a gap that was too wide. He missed his branch, clawed at some leaves, and came tumbling to the ground. The second squirrel went to dancing up and down on his branch then, chattering louder than ever. It was plain that he was getting a big laugh out of how that show-off squirrel had made such a fool of himself.

The sight was so funny that I laughed, myself, and that's where I made my mistake.

Where the doe had come from and how she ever got so close without my seeing her, I don't know. It was like she'd suddenly lit down out of the air like a buzzard or risen right up out of the bare ground around the rocks. Anyhow, there she stood, staring straight at me, sniffing and snorting and stomping her forefeet against the ground.

She couldn't have scented me, and I hadn't moved; but I had laughed out loud a little at those squirrels. And that sound had warned her.

Well, I couldn't lift my gun then, with her staring straight at me. She'd see the motion and take a scare. And while Papa was a good enough shot to down a running deer, I'd never tried it and didn't much think I could. I figured it smarter to wait. Maybe she'd quit staring at me after a while and give me a chance to lift my gun.

But I waited and waited, and still she kept looking at me, trying to figure me out. Finally, she started coming toward me. She'd take one dancing step and then another and bob her head and flap her long ears about, then start moving toward me again.

I didn't know what to do. It made me nervous, the way she kept coming at me. Sooner or later she was bound to make out what I was. Then she'd whirl and be gone before I could draw a bead on her.

She kept doing me that way till finally my heart was flopping around inside my chest like a catfish in a wet sack. I could feel my muscles tightening up all over. I knew then that I couldn't wait any longer. It was either shoot or bust wide open, so I whipped my gun up to my shoulder.

Like I'd figured, she snorted and wheeled, so fast that she was just a brown blur against my gunsights. I pressed the trigger, hoping my aim was good.

After I fired, the black powder charge in my gun threw up such a thick fog of blue smoke that I couldn't see through it. I reloaded, then leaped to my feet and went running through the smoke. What I saw when I came into the clear again made my heart drop down into my shoes.

There went the frightened, snorting cattle, stampeding through the trees with their tails in the air like it was heel-fly time. And right beside them went my doe, running all humped up and with her white, pointed tail clamped tight to her rump.

Which meant that I'd hit her but hadn't made a killing shot.

I didn't like that. I never minded killing for meat. Like Papa had told me, every creature has to kill to live. But to wound an animal was something else. Especially one as pretty and harmless as a deer. It made me sick to think of the doe's escaping, maybe to hurt for days before she finally died.

I swung my gun up, hoping yet to get in a

killing shot. But I couldn't fire on account of the cattle. They were too close to the deer. I might kill one of them.

Then suddenly the doe did a surprising thing. 'Way down in the flat there, nearly out of sight, she ran head on into the trunk of a tree. Like she was stone blind. I saw the flash of her light-colored belly as she went down. I waited. She didn't get up. I tore out, running through the chin-tall grass as fast as I could.

When finally I reached the place, all out of breath, I found her lying dead, with a bullet hole through her middle, right where it had to have shattered the heart.

Suddenly I wasn't sick any more. I felt big and strong and sure of myself. I hadn't made a bad shot. I hadn't caused an animal a lot of suffering. All I'd done was get meat for the family, shooting it on the run, just like Papa did.

I rode toward the cabin, sitting behind the gutted doe that I'd tied across Jumper's back. I rode, feeling proud of myself as a hunter and a provider for the family. Making a killing shot like that on a moving deer made me feel bigger and more important. Too big and important, I guessed, to fuss with Little Arliss about that old yeller dog. I still didn't think much of the idea of keeping him, but I guessed that when you are nearly a man, you have to learn to put up with a lot of aggravation from little old bitty kids. Let Arliss keep the thieving rascal. I guessed I could provide enough meat for him, too.

That's how I was feeling when I crossed Birdsong Creek and rode up to the spring under the trees below the house. Then suddenly, I felt different. That's when I found Little Arliss in the pool again. And in there with him was the big yeller dog. That dirty stinking rascal, romping around in our drinking water!

"Arliss!" I yelled at Little Arliss. "You get that nasty old dog out of the water!"

They hadn't seen me ride up, and I guess it was my sudden yell that surprised them both so bad. Arliss went tearing out of the pool on one side and the dog on the other. Arliss was screaming his head off, and here came the big dog with his wet fur rising along the ridge of his backbone, baying me like I was a panther.

I didn't give him a chance to get to me. I was too quick about jumping off the mule and grabbing up some rocks.

I was lucky. The first rock I threw caught

the big dog right between the eyes, and I was throwing hard. He went down, yelling and pitching and wallowing. And just as he came to his feet again, I caught him in the ribs with another one. That was too much for him. He turned tail then and took out for the house, squawling and bawling.

But I wasn't the only good rock thrower in the family. Arliss was only five years old, but I'd spent a lot of time showing him how to throw a rock. Now I wished I hadn't. Because about then, a rock nearly tore my left ear off. I whirled around just barely in time to duck another that would have caught me square in the left eye.

I yelled, "Arliss, you quit that!" but Arliss wasn't listening. He was too scared and too mad. He bent over to pick up a rock big enough to brain me with if he'd been strong enough to throw it.

Well, when you're fourteen years old, you can't afford to mix in a rock fight with your five-year-old brother. You can't do it, even when you're in the right. You just can't explain a thing like that to your folks. All they'll do is point out how much bigger you are, how unfair it is to your little brother.

All I could do was turn tail like the yeller dog and head for the house, yelling for

Mama. And right after me came Little Arliss, naked and running as fast as he could, doing his dead-level best to get close enough to hit me with the big rock he was packing.

I outran him, of course; and then here came Mama, running so fast that her long skirts were flying, and calling out: "What on earth, boys!"

I hollered, "You better catch that Arliss!" as I ran past her. And she did; but Little Arliss was so mad that I thought for a second he was going to hit her with the rock before she could get it away from him.

Well, it all wound up about like I figured. Mama switched Little Arliss for playing in our drinking water. Then she blessed me out good and proper for being so bossy with him. And the big yeller dog that had caused all the trouble got off scot free.

It didn't seem right and fair to me. How could I be the man of the family if nobody paid any attention to what I thought or said?

I went and led Jumper up to the house. I hung the doe in the liveoak tree that grew beside the house and began skinning it and cutting up the meat. I thought of the fine shot I'd made and knew it was worth bragging about to Mama. But what was the use? She wouldn't pay me any mind—not until I did something she thought I shouldn't have done. Then she'd treat me like I wasn't any older than Little Arliss.

I sulked and felt sorry for myself all the time I worked with the meat. The more I thought about it, the madder I got at the big yeller dog.

I hung the fresh cuts of venison up in the dog run, right where Old Yeller had stolen the hog meat the night he came. I did it for a couple of reasons. To begin with, that was the handiest and coolest place we had for hanging fresh meat. On top of that, I was looking for a good excuse to get rid of that dog. I figured if he stole more of our meat, Mama would have to see that he was too sorry and no account to keep.

But Old Yeller was too smart for that. He gnawed around on some of the deer's leg bones that Mama threw away; but not once did he ever even act like he could smell the meat we'd hung up.

FOUR

A couple of days later, I had another and better reason for wanting to get rid of Old Yeller. That was when the two longhorn range bulls met at the house and pulled off their big fight.

We first heard the bulls while we were eating our dinner of cornbread, roasted venison, and green watercress gathered from below the spring. One bull came from off a high rocky ridge to the south of the cabin. We could hear his angry rumbling as he moved down through the thickets of catclaw and scrub oak.

Then he lifted his voice in a wild brassy

blare that set echoes clamoring in the draws and canyons for miles around.

"That old bull's talking fight," I told Mama and Little Arliss. "He's bragging that he's the biggest and toughest and meanest. He's telling all the other bulls that if they've got a lick of sense, they'll take to cover when he's around."

Almost before I'd finished talking, we heard the second bull. He was over about the Salt Licks somewhere. His bellering was just as loud and braggy as the first one's. He was telling the first bull that his fight talk was all bluff. He was saying that *he* was the he bull of the range, that *he* was the biggest and meanest and toughest.

We sat and ate and listened to them. We could tell by their rumblings and bawlings that they were gradually working their way down through the brush toward each other and getting madder by the minute.

I always liked to see a fight between bulls or bears or wild boars or almost any wild animals. Now, I got so excited that I jumped up from the table and went to the door and stood listening. I'd made up my mind that if the bulls met and started a fight, I was going to see it. There was still plenty of careless weeds and crabgrass that needed hoeing out of the corn, but I guessed I could let them go long enough to see a bullfight.

Our cabin stood on a high knoll about a hundred yards above the spring. Years ago, Papa had cleared out all the brush and trees from around it, leaving a couple of liveoaks near the house for shade. That was so he could get a clear shot at any Comanche or Apache coming to scalp us. And while I stood there at the door, the first bull entered the clearing, right where Papa had one time shot a Comanche off his horse.

He was a leggy, mustard-colored bull with black freckles speckling his jaws and the underside of his belly. He had one great horn set for hooking, while the other hung down past his jaw like a tallow candle that had drooped in the heat. He was what the Mexicans called a *chongo* or "droop horn."

He trotted out a little piece into the clearing, then stopped to drop his head low. He went to snorting and shaking his horns and pawing up the dry dirt with his forefeet. He flung the dirt back over his neck and shoulders in great clouds of dust.

I couldn't see the other bull yet, but I could tell by the sound of him that he was close and coming in a trot. I hollered back to Mama and Little Arliss.

"They're fixing to fight right here, where we can all see it."

There was a split-rail fence around our cabin. I ran out and climbed up and took a seat on the top rail. Mama and Little Arliss came and climbed up to sit beside me.

Then, from the other side of the clearing came the second bull. He was the red roan I'd seen at the Salt Licks the day I shot the doe. He wasn't as tall and longlegged as the *chongo* bull, but every bit as heavy and powerful. And while his horns were shorter, they were both curved right for hooking.

Like the first bull, he came blaring out into the clearing, then stopped, to snort and sling his wicked horns and paw up clouds of dust. He made it plain that he wanted to fight just as bad as the first bull.

About that time, from somewhere behind the cabin, came Old Yeller. He charged through the rails, bristled up and roaring almost as loud as the bulls. All their bellering and snorting and dust pawing sounded like a threat to him. He'd come out to run them away from the house.

I hollered at him. "Get back there, you rascal," I shouted. "You're fixing to spoil our show."

That stopped him, but he still wasn't satisfied. He kept baying the bulls till I jumped down and picked up a rock. I didn't have to throw it. All I had to do was draw back like I was going to. That sent him flying back into the yard and around the corner of the cabin, yelling like I'd murdered him.

That also put Little Arliss on the fight.

He started screaming at me. He tried to get down where he could pick up a rock.

But Mama held him. "Hush, now, baby," she said. "Travis isn't going to hurt your dog. He just doesn't want him to scare off the bulls."

Well, it took some talking, but she finally got Little Arliss's mind off hitting me with a rock. I climbed back up on the fence. I told Mama that I was betting on Chongo. She said she was betting her money on Roany because he had two fighting horns. We sat there and watched the bulls get ready to fight and talked and laughed and had ourselves a real good time. We never once thought about being in any danger.

When we learned different, it was nearly too late.

Suddenly, Chongo quit pawing the dirt and flung his tail into the air.

"Look out!" I shouted. "Here it comes."

Sure enough, Chongo charged, pounding

the hardpan with his feet and roaring his mightiest. And here came Roany to meet him, charging with his head low and his tail high in the air.

I let out an excited yell. They met head on, with a loud crash of horns and a jar so solid that it seemed like I could feel it clear up there on the fence. Roany went down. I yelled louder, thinking Chongo was winning.

A second later, though, Roany was back on his feet and charging through the cloud of dust their hoofs had churned up. He caught Chongo broadside. He slammed his sharp horns up to the hilt in the shoulder of the mustard-colored bull. He drove against him so fast and hard that Chongo couldn't wheel away. All he could do was barely keep on his feet by giving ground.

And here they came, straight for our rail fence.

"Land sakes!" Mama cried suddenly and leaped from the fence, dragging Little Arliss down after her.

But I was too excited about the fight. I didn't see the danger in time. I was still astride the top rail when the struggling bulls crashed through the fence, splintering the posts and rails, and toppling me to the ground almost under them.

I lunged to my feet, wild with scare, and got knocked flat on my face in the dirt.

I sure thought I was a goner. The roaring of the bulls was right in my ears. The hot, reeking scent of their blood was in my nose. The bone-crashing weight of their hoofs was stomping all around and over me, churning up such a fog of dust that I couldn't see a thing.

Then suddenly Mama had me by the hand and was dragging me out from under, yelling in a scared voice: "Run, Travis, run!"

Well, she didn't have to keep hollering at me. I was running as fast as I ever hoped to run. And with her running faster and dragging me along by the hand, we scooted through the open cabin door just about a quick breath before Roany slammed Chongo against it.

They hit so hard that the whole cabin shook. I saw great big chunks of dried-mud chinking fall from between the logs. There for a second, I thought Chongo was coming through that door, right on top of us. But turned broadside like he was, he was too big to be shoved through such a small opening. Then a second later, he got off Roany's horns somehow and wheeled on him. Here they went, then, down alongside the cabin wall, roaring and stomping and slamming their heels against the logs.

I looked at Mama and Little Arliss. Mama's face was white as a bed sheet. For once, Little Arliss was so scared that he couldn't scream. Suddenly, I wasn't scared anymore. I was just plain mad.

I reached for a braided rawhide whip that hung in a coil on a wooden peg driven between the logs.

That scared Mama still worse. "Oh, no, Travis," she cried. "Don't go out there!"

"They're fixing to tear down the house, Mama," I said.

"But they might run over you," Mama argued.

The bulls crashed into the cabin again. They grunted and strained and roared. Their horns and hoofs clattered against the logs.

I turned and headed for the door. Looked to me like they'd kill us all if they ever broke through those log walls.

Mama came running to grab me by the arm. "Call the dog!" she said. "Put the dog after them!"

Well, that was a real good idea. I was half aggravated with myself because I hadn't thought of it. Here was a chance for the old yeller dog to pay back for all the trouble he'd made around the place.

I stuck my head out the door. The bulls had fought away from the house. Now they were busy tearing down more of the yard fence.

I ducked out and around the corner. I ran through the dog run toward the back of the house, calling, "Here, Yeller! Here, Yeller! Get 'em, boy! Sic 'em!"

Old Yeller was back there, all right. But he didn't come and he didn't sic 'em. He took one look at me running toward him with that bullwhip in my hand and knew I'd come to kill him. He tucked his tail and lit out in a yelling run for the woods.

If there had been any way I could have done it, right then is when I would have killed him.

But there wasn't time to mess with a fool dog. I had to do something about those bulls. They were wrecking the place, and I had to stop it. Papa had left me to look after things while he was gone, and I wasn't about to let two mad bulls tear up everything we had.

I ran up to the bulls and went to work on them with the whip. It was a heavy sixteen-footer and I'd practiced with it a lot. I could crack that rawhide popper louder than a gunshot. I could cut a branch as thick as my little finger off a green mesquite with it.

But I couldn't stop those bulls from fighting. They were too mad. They were hurting too much already; I might as well have been spitting on them. I yelled and whipped them till I gave clear out. Still they went right on with their roaring bloody battle.

I guess they would have kept on fighting till they leveled the house to the ground if it hadn't been for a freak accident.

We had a heavy two-wheeled Mexican cart that Papa used for hauling wood and hay. It happened to be standing out in front of the house, right where the ground broke away in a sharp slant toward the spring and creek.

It had just come to me that I could get my gun and shoot the bulls when Chongo crowded Roany up against the cart. He ran that long single horn clear under Roany's belly. Now he gave such a big heave that he lifted Roany's feet clear off the ground and rolled him in the air. A second later, Roany landed flat on his back inside the bed of that dump cart, with all four feet sticking up.

I thought his weight would break the cart to pieces, but I was wrong. The cart was stronger than I'd thought. All the bull's weight did was tilt it so that the wheels started rolling. And away the cart went down the hill, carrying Roany with it.

When that happened, Chongo was suddenly the silliest-looking bull you ever saw. He stood with his tail up and his head high, staring after the runaway cart. He couldn't for the life of him figure out what he'd done with the roan bull.

The rolling cart rattled and banged and careened its way down the slope till it was right beside the spring. There, one wheel struck a big boulder, bouncing that side of the cart so high that it turned over and skidded to a stop. The roan bull spilled right into the spring. Water flew in all directions.

Roany got his feet under him. He scrambled up out of the hole. But I guess that cart ride and sudden wetting had taken all the fight out of him. Anyhow, he headed for the timber, running with his tail tucked. Water streamed down out of his hair, leaving a dark wet trail in the dry dust to show which way he'd gone.

Chongo saw Roany then. He snorted and went after him. But when he got to the cart, he slid to a sudden stop. The cart, lying on its side now, still had that top wheel spinning around and around. Chongo had never seen anything like that. He stood and stared at the spinning wheel. He couldn't understand it. He lifted his nose up close to smell it. Finally he reached out a long tongue to lick and taste it.

That was a bad mistake. I guess the iron tire on the spinning wheel was roughed up pretty badly and maybe had chips of broken rock and gravel stuck to it. Anyhow, from the way Chongo acted, it must have scraped all the hide off his tongue.

Chongo bawled and went running backward. He whirled away so fast that he lost his footing and fell down. He came to his feet and took out in the opposite direction from the roan bull. He ran, slinging his head and flopping his long tongue around, bawling like he'd stuck it into a bear trap. He ran with his tail clamped just as tight as the roan bull's.

It was enough to make you laugh your head off, the way both of those bad bulls had gotten the wits scared clear out of them, each one thinking he'd lost the fight.

But they sure had made a wreck of the yard fence.

FIVE

That Little Arliss! If he wasn't a mess! From the time he'd grown up big enough to get out of the cabin, he'd made a practice of trying to catch and keep every living thing that ran, flew, jumped, or crawled.

Every night before Mama let him go to bed, she'd make Arliss empty his pockets of whatever he'd captured during the day. Generally, it would be a tangled-up mess of grasshoppers and worms and praying bugs and little rusty tree lizards. One time he brought in a horned toad that got so mad he swelled out round and flat as a Mexican *tortilla* and bled at the eyes. Sometimes it was stuff like a young bird that had fallen out of its nest before it could fly, or a green-speckled spring frog or a striped water snake. And once he turned out of his pocket a wadded-up baby copperhead that nearly threw Mama into spasms. We never did figure out why the snake hadn't bitten him, but Mama took no more chances on snakes. She switched Arliss hard for catching that snake. Then she made me spend better than a week, taking him out and teaching him to throw rocks and kill snakes.

That was all right with Little Arliss. If Mama wanted him to kill his snakes first, he'd kill them. But that still didn't keep him from sticking them in his pockets along with everything else he'd captured that day. The snakes might be stinking by the time Mama called on him to empty his pockets, but they'd be dead.

Then, after the yeller dog came, Little Arliss started catching even bigger game. Like cottontail rabbits and chaparral birds and a baby possum that sulked and lay like dead for the first several hours until he finally decided that Arliss wasn't going to hurt him.

Of course, it was Old Yeller that was doing the catching. He'd run the game down and turn it over to Little Arliss. Then Little Arliss could come in and tell Mama a big fib about how he caught it himself.

I watched them one day when they caught a blue catfish out of Birdsong Creek. The fish had fed out into water so shallow that his top fin was sticking out. About the time I saw it, Old Yeller and Little Arliss did, too. They made a run at it. The fish went scooting away toward deeper water, only Yeller was too fast for him. He pounced on the fish and shut his big mouth down over it and went romping to the bank, where he dropped it down on the grass and let it flop. And here came Little Arliss to fall on it like I guess he'd been doing everything else. The minute he got his hands on it, the fish finned him and he went to crying.

But he wouldn't turn the fish loose. He just grabbed it up and went running and squawling toward the house, where he gave the fish to Mama. His hands were all bloody by then, where the fish had finned him. They swelled up and got mighty sore; not even a mesquite thorn hurts as bad as a sharp fish fin when it's run deep into your hand.

But as soon as Mama had wrapped his hands in a poultice of mashed-up prickly-pear root to draw out the poison, Little Ar-

49

liss forgot all about his hurt. And that night when we ate the fish for supper, he told the biggest windy I ever heard about how he'd dived 'way down into a deep hole under the rocks and dragged that fish out and nearly got drowned before he could swim to the bank with it.

But when I tried to tell Mama what really happened, she wouldn't let me. "Now, this is Arliss's story," she said. "You let him tell it the way he wants to."

I told Mama then, I said: "Mama, that old yeller dog is going to make the biggest liar in Texas out of Little Arliss."

But Mama just laughed at me, like she always laughed at Little Arliss's big windies after she'd gotten off where he couldn't hear her. She said for me to let Little Arliss alone. She said that if he ever told a bigger whopper than the ones I used to tell, she had yet to hear it.

Well, I hushed then. If Mama wanted Little Arliss to grow up to be the biggest liar in Texas, I guessed it wasn't any of my business.

All of which, I figure, is what led up to Little Arliss's catching the bear. I think Mama had let him tell so many big yarns about his catching live game that he'd begun to believe them himself.

When it happened, I was down the creek a ways, splitting rails to fix up the yard fence where the bulls had torn it down. I'd been down there since dinner, working in a stand of tall slim post oaks. I'd chop down a tree, trim off the branches as far up as I wanted, then cut away the rest of the top. After that I'd start splitting the log.

I'd split the log by driving steel wedges into the wood. I'd start at the big end and hammer in a wedge with the back side of my axe. This would start a little split running lengthways of the log. Then I'd take a second wedge and drive it into this split. This would split the log further along and, at the same time, loosen the first wedge. I'd then knock the first wedge loose and move it up in front of the second one.

Driving one wedge ahead of the other like that, I could finally split a log in two halves. Then I'd go to work on the halves, splitting them apart. That way, from each log, I'd come out with four rails.

Swinging that chopping axe was sure hard work. The sweat poured off me. My back muscles ached. The axe got so heavy I could hardly swing it. My breath got harder and harder to breathe.

An hour before sundown, I was worn down to a nub. It seemed like I couldn't hit another lick. Papa could have lasted till past sundown, but I didn't see how I could. I shouldered my axe and started toward the cabin, trying to think up some excuse to tell Mama to keep her from knowing I was played clear out.

That's when I heard Little Arliss scream.

Well, Little Arliss was a screamer by nature. He'd scream when he was happy and scream when he was mad and a lot of times he'd scream just to hear himself make a noise. Generally, we paid no more mind to his screaming than we did to the gobble of a wild turkey.

But this time was different. The second I heard his screaming, I felt my heart flop clear over. This time I knew Little Arliss was in real trouble.

I tore out up the trail leading toward the cabin. A minute before, I'd been so tired out with my rail splitting that I couldn't have struck a trot. But now I raced through the tall trees in that creek bottom, covering ground like a scared wolf.

Little Arliss's second scream, when it came, was louder and shriller and more frantic-sounding than the first. Mixed with it was a whimpering crying sound that I knew didn't come from him. It was a sound I'd heard before and seemed like I ought to know what it was, but right then I couldn't place it.

Then, from way off to one side came a sound that I would have recognized anywhere. It was the coughing roar of a charging bear. I'd just heard it once in my life. That was the time Mama had shot and wounded a hog-killing bear and Papa had had to finish it off with a knife to keep it from getting her.

My heart went to pushing up into my throat, nearly choking off my wind. I strained for every lick of speed I could get out of my running legs. I didn't know what sort of fix Little Arliss had got himself into, but I knew that it had to do with a mad bear, which was enough.

The way the late sun slanted through the trees had the trail all cross-banded with streaks of bright light and dark shade. I ran through these bright and dark patches so fast that the changing light nearly blinded me. Then suddenly, I raced out into the open where I could see ahead. And what I saw sent a chill clear through to the marrow of my bones.

There was Little Arliss, down in that spring hole again. He was lying half in and half out of the water, holding onto the hind leg of a little black bear cub no bigger than a small coon. The bear cub was out on the bank, whimpering and crying and clawing the rocks with all three of his other feet, trying to pull away. But Little Arliss was holding on for all he was worth, scared now and screaming his head off. Too scared to let go.

How the bear cub ever came to prowl close enough for Little Arliss to grab him, I don't know. And why he didn't turn on him and bite loose, I couldn't figure out, either. Unless he was like Little Arliss, too scared to think.

But all of that didn't matter now. What mattered was the bear cub's mama. She'd heard the cries of her baby and was coming to save him. She was coming so fast that she had the brush popping and breaking as she crashed through and over it. I could see her black heavy figure piling off down the slant on the far side of Birdsong Creek. She was roaring mad and ready to kill.

And worst of all, I could see that I'd never get there in time!

Mama couldn't either. She'd heard Arliss, too, and here she came from the cabin, running down the slant toward the spring, screaming at Arliss, telling him to turn the bear cub loose. But Little Arliss wouldn't do it. All he'd do was hang with that hind leg and let out one shrill shriek after another as fast as he could suck in a breath.

Now the she bear was charging across the shallows in the creek. She was knocking sheets of water high in the bright sun, charging with her fur up and her long teeth bared, filling the canyon with that awful coughing roar. And no matter how fast Mama ran or how fast I ran, the she bear was going to get there first!

I think I nearly went blind then, picturing what was going to happen to Little Arliss. I know that I opened my mouth to scream and not any sound came out.

Then, just as the bear went lunging up the creek bank toward Little Arliss and her cub, a flash of yellow came streaking out of the brush.

It was that big yeller dog. He was roaring like a mad bull. He wasn't one-third as big and heavy as the she bear, but when he piled into her from one side, he rolled her clear off her feet. They went down in a wild, roaring tangle of twisting bodies and scrambling feet and slashing fangs.

As I raced past them, I saw the bear lunge up to stand on her hind feet like a man while she clawed at the body of the yeller dog hanging to her throat. I didn't wait to see more. Without ever checking my stride, I ran in and jerked Little Arliss loose from the cub. I grabbed him by the wrist and yanked him up out of that water and slung him toward Mama like he was a half-empty sack of corn. I screamed at Mama. "Grab him, Mama! Grab him and run!" Then I swung my chopping axe high and wheeled, aiming to cave in the she bear's head with the first lick.

But I never did strike. I didn't need to. Old Yeller hadn't let the bear get close enough. He couldn't handle her; she was too big and strong for that. She'd stand there on her hind feet, hunched over, and take a roaring swing at him with one of those big front claws. She'd slap him head over heels. She'd knock him so far that it didn't look like he could possibly get back there before she charged again, but he always did. He'd hit the ground rolling, yelling his head off with the pain of the blow; but somehow he'd always roll to his feet. And here he'd come again, ready to tie into her for another round.

I stood there with my axe raised, watching them for a long moment. Then from up toward the house, I heard Mama calling: "Come away from there, Travis. Hurry, son! Run!"

That spooked me. Up till then, I'd been ready to tie into that bear myself. Now, suddenly, I was scared out of my wits again. I ran toward the cabin.

But like it was, Old Yeller nearly beat me there. I didn't see it, of course; but Mama said that the minute Old Yeller saw we were all in the clear and out of danger, he threw the fight to that she bear and lit out for the house. The bear chased him for a little piece, but at the rate Old Yeller was leaving her behind, Mama said it looked like the bear was backing up.

But if the big yeller dog was scared or hurt in any way when he came dashing into the house, he didn't show it. He sure didn't show it like we all did. Little Arliss had hushed his screaming, but he was trembling all over and clinging to Mama like he'd never let her go. And Mama was sitting in the middle of the floor, holding him up close and crying like she'd never stop. And me, I was close to crying, myself.

Old Yeller, though, all he did was come bounding in to jump on us and lick us in the face and bark so loud that there, inside the cabin, the noise nearly made us deaf.

The way he acted, you might have thought that bear fight hadn't been anything more than a rowdy romp that we'd all taken part in for the fun of it.

SIX

Till Little Arliss got us mixed up in that bear fight, I guess I'd been looking on him about like most boys look on their little brothers. I liked him, all right, but I didn't have a lot of use for him. What with his always playing in our drinking water and getting in the way of my chopping axe and howling his head off and chunking me with rocks when he got mad, it didn't seem to me like he was hardly worth the bother of putting up with.

But that day when I saw him in the spring, so helpless against the angry she bear, I learned different. I knew then that I loved him as much as I did Mama and Papa, maybe in some ways even a little bit more.

So it was only natural for me to come to love the dog that saved him.

After that, I couldn't do enough for Old Yeller. What if he was a big ugly meat-stealing rascal? What if he did fall over and yell bloody murder every time I looked crossways at him? What if he had run off when he ought to have helped with the fighting bulls? None of that made a lick of difference now. He'd pitched in and saved Little Arliss when I couldn't possibly have done it, and that was enough for me.

I petted him and made over him till he was wiggling all over to show how happy he was. I felt mean about how I'd treated him and did everything I could to let him know. I searched his feet and pulled out a long mesquite thorn that had become embedded between his toes. I held him down and had Mama hand me a stick with a coal of fire on it, so I could burn off three big bloated ticks that I found inside one of his ears. I washed him with lye soap and water, then rubbed salty bacon grease into his hair all over to rout the fleas. And that night after dark, when he sneaked into bed with me and Little Arliss, I let him sleep there and never said a word about it to Mama.

I took him and Little Arliss squirrel hunting the next day. It was the first time I'd ever taken Little Arliss on any kind of hunt. He was such a noisy pest that I always figured he'd scare off the game.

As it turned out, he was just as noisy and pesky as I'd figured. He'd follow along, keeping quiet like I told him, till he saw maybe a pretty butterfly floating around in the air. Then he'd set up a yell you could have heard a mile off and go chasing after the butterfly. Of course, he couldn't catch it; but he would keep yelling at me to come help him. Then he'd get mad because I wouldn't and yell still louder. Or maybe he'd stop to turn over a flat rock. Then he'd stand yelling at me to come back and look at all the yellow ants and centipedes and crickets and stinging scorpions that went scurrying away, hunting new hiding places.

Once he got hung up in some briars and yelled till I came back to get him out. Another time he fell down and struck his elbow on a rock and didn't say a word about it for several minutes—until he saw blood seeping out of a cut on his arm. Then he stood and screamed like he was being burnt with a hot iron.

With that much racket going on, I knew we'd scare all the game clear out of the country. Which, I guess we did. All but the squirrels. They took to the trees where they could hide from us. But I was lucky enough to see which tree one squirrel went up; so I put some of Little Arliss's racket to use.

I sent him in a circle around the tree, beating on the grass and bushes with a stick, while I stood waiting. Sure enough, the squirrel got to watching Little Arliss and forgot me. He kept turning around the tree limb to keep it between him and Little Arliss, till he was on my side in plain sight. I shot him out of the tree the first shot.

After that, Old Yeller caught onto what game we were after. He went to work then, trailing and treeing the squirrels that Little Arliss was scaring up off the ground. From then on, with Yeller to tree the squirrels and Little Arliss to turn them on the tree limbs, we had pickings. Wasn't but a little bit till I'd shot five, more than enough to make us a good squirrel fry for supper.

A week later, Old Yeller helped me catch a wild gobbler that I'd have lost without him. We had gone up to the corn patch to pick a bait of blackeyed peas. I was packing my gun. Just as we got up to the slabrock fence that Papa had built around the corn patch, I looked over and spotted this gobbler doing our pea-picking for us. The pea pods were still green yet, most of them no further along than snapping size. This made them hard for the gobbler to shell, but he was working away at it, pecking and scratching so hard that he was raising a big dust out in the field.

"Why, that old rascal," Mama said. "He's just clawing those pea vines all to pieces."

"Hush, Mama," I said. "Don't scare him." I lifted my gun and laid the barrel across the top of the rock fence. "I'll have him ready for the pot in just a minute."

It wasn't a long shot, and I had him sighted in, dead to rights. I aimed to stick a bullet right where his wings hinged to his back. I was holding my breath and already squeezing off when Little Arliss, who'd gotten behind, came running up.

"Whatcha shootin' at, Travis?" he yelled at the top of his voice. "Whatcha shootin' at?"

Well, that made me and the gobbler both jump. The gun fired, and I saw the gobbler go down. But a second later, he was up again, streaking through the tall corn, dragging a broken wing.

For a second, I was so mad at Little Arliss I could have wrung his neck like a frying chicken's. I said, "*Arliss!* Why can't you keep your mouth shut? You've made me lose that gobbler!"

Well, Little Arliss didn't have sense enough to know what I was mad about. Right away, he puckered up and went to crying and leaking tears all over the place. Some of them splattered clear down on his bare feet, making dark splotches in the dust that covered them. I always did say that when Little Arliss cried he could shed more tears faster than any crier I ever saw.

"Wait a minute!" Mama put in. "I don't think you've lost your gobbler yet. Look yonder!"

She pointed, and I looked, and there was Old Yeller jumping the rock fence and racing toward the pea patch. He ran up to where I'd knocked the gobbler down. He circled the place one time, smelling the ground and wiggling his stub tail. Then he took off through the corn the same way the gobbler went, yelling like I was beating him with a stick.

When he barked treed a couple of minutes later, it was in the woods the other side of the corn patch. We went to him. We found him jumping at the gobbler that had run up a stooping liveoak and was perched there, panting, just waiting for me.

So in spite of the fact that Little Arliss had caused me to make a bad shot, we had us a real sumptuous supper that night. Roast turkey with cornbread dressing and watercress and wild onions that Little Arliss and I found growing down in the creek next to the water.

But when we tried to feed Old Yeller some of the turkey, on account of his saving us from losing it, he wouldn't eat. He'd lick the meat and wiggle his stub tail to show how grateful he was, but he didn't swallow down more than a bite or two.

That puzzled Mama and me because, when we remembered back, we realized that he hadn't been eating anything we'd fed him for the last several days. Yet he was fat and with hair as slick and shiny as a dog eating three square meals a day.

Mama shook her head. "If I didn't know better," she said, "I'd say that dog was sucking eggs. But I've got three hens setting and one with biddy chickens, and I'm getting more eggs from the rest of them than I've gotten since last fall. So he can't be robbing the nests."

Well, we wondered some about what Old Yeller was living on, but didn't worry about it. That is, not until the day Bud Searcy dropped by the cabin to see how we were making out.

Bud Searcy was a red-faced man with a bulging middle who liked to visit around the settlement and sit and talk hard times and spit tobacco juice all over the place and wait for somebody to ask him to dinner.

I never did have a lot of use for him and my folks didn't, either. Mama said he was shiftless. She said that was the reason the rest of the men left him at home to sort of look after the womenfolks and kids while they were gone on the cow drive. She said the men knew that if they took Bud Searcy along, they'd never get to Kansas before the steers were dead with old age. It would take Searcy that long to get through visiting and eating with everybody between Salt Licks and Abilene.

But he did have a little white-haired granddaughter that I sort of liked. She was eleven and different from most girls. She would hang around and watch what boys did, like showing how high they could climb in a tree or how far they could throw a rock

66

or how fast they could swim or how good they could shoot. But she never wanted to mix in or try to take over and boss things. She just went along and watched and didn't say much, and the only thing I had against her was her eyes. They were big solemn brown eyes and right pretty to look at; only when she fixed them on me, it always seemed like they looked clear through me and saw everything I was thinking. That always made me sort of jumpy, so that when I could, I never would look right straight at her.

Her name was Lisbeth and she came with her grandpa the day he visited us. They came riding up on an old shad-bellied pony that didn't look like he'd had a fill of corn in a coon's age. She rode behind her grandpa's saddle, holding to his belt in the back, and her white hair was all curly and rippling in the sun. Trotting behind them was a blue-ticked she dog that I always figured was one of Bell's pups.

Old Yeller went out to bay them as they rode up. I noticed right off that he didn't go about it like he really meant business. His yelling bay sounded a lot more like he was just barking because he figured that's what we expected him to do. And the first time I hollered at him, telling him to dry up all that racket, he hushed. Which surprised me, as hard-headed as he generally was.

By the time Mama had come to the door and told Searcy and Lisbeth to get down and come right in, Old Yeller had started a romp with the blue-ticked bitch.

Lisbeth slipped to the ground and stood staring at me with those big solemn eyes while her grandpa dismounted. Searcy told Mama that he believed he wouldn't come in the house. He said that as hot as the day was, he figured he'd like it better sitting in the dog run. So Mama had me bring out our four cowhide bottom chairs. Searcy picked the one I always liked to sit in best. He got out a twist of tobacco and bit off a chew big enough to bulge his cheek and went to chewing and talking and spitting juice right where we'd all be bound to step in it and pack it around on the bottoms of our feet.

First he asked Mama if we were making out all right, and Mama said we were. Then he told her that he'd been left to look after all the families while the men were gone, a mighty heavy responsibility that was nearly working him to death, but that he was glad to do it. He said for Mama to remember that if the least little thing went wrong, she was to get in touch with him right away. And Mama said she would.

Then he leaned his chair back against the cabin wall and went on telling what all was going on around in the settlement. He told about how dry the weather was and how he looked for all the corn crops to fail and the settlement folks to be scraping the bottoms of their meal barrels long before next spring. He told how the cows were going dry and the gardens were failing. He told how Jed Simpson's boy Rosal was sitting at a turkey roost, waiting for a shot, when a fox came right up and tried to jump on him, and Rosal had to club it to death with his gun butt. This sure looked like a case of hydrophobia to Searcy, as anybody knew that no fox in his right mind was going to jump on a hunter.

Which reminded him of an uncle of his that got mad-dog bit down in the piney woods of East Texas. This was 'way back when Searcy was a little boy. As soon as the dog bit him, the man knew he was bound to die; so he went and got a big log chain and tied one end around the bottom of a tree and the other one to one of his legs. And right there he stayed till the sickness got him and he lost his mind. He slobbered at the mouth and moaned and screamed and ran at his wife and children, trying to catch them and bite them. Only, of course, the chain around his leg held him back, which was the reason he'd chained himself to the tree in the first place. And right there, chained to that tree, he finally died and they buried him under the same tree.

Bud Searcy sure hoped that we wouldn't have an outbreak of hydrophobia in Salt Licks and all die before the men got back from Kansas.

Then he talked awhile about a panther that had caught and killed one of Joe Anson's colts and how the Anson boys had put their dogs on the trail. They ran the panther into the cave and Jeff Anson followed in where the dogs had more sense than to go and got pretty badly panther-mauled for his trouble; but he did get the panther.

Searcy talked till dinnertime, said not a word all through dinner, and then went back to talking as quick as he'd swallowed down the last bite.

He told how some strange varmint that wasn't a coyote, possum, skunk, or coon had recently started robbing the settlement blind. Or maybe it was even some*body*. Nobody could tell for sure. All they knew was that they were losing meat out of their smokehouses, eggs out of their hens' nests, and sometimes even whole pans of cornbread that the womenfolks had set out to cool. Ike Fuller had been barbecuing some meat over an open pit and left it for a minute to go get a drink of water and came back to find that a three- or four-pound chunk of beef ribs had disappeared like it had gone up in smoke.

Salt Licks folks were getting pretty riled about it, Searcy said, and guessed it would go hard with whatever or whoever was doing the raiding if they ever learned what it was.

Listening to this, I got an uneasy feeling. The feeling got worse a minute later when Lisbeth motioned me to follow her off down to the spring.

We walked clear down there, with Old Yeller and the blue-tick dog following with us, before she finally looked up at me and said, "It's him."

"What do you mean?" I said.

"I mean it's your big yeller dog," she said. "I saw him."

"Do what?" I asked.

"Steal that bait of ribs," she said. "I saw

71

him get a bunch of eggs, too. From one of our nests."

I stopped then and looked straight at her and she looked straight back at me and I couldn't stand it and had to look down.

"But I'm not going to tell," she said.

I didn't believe her. "I bet you do," I said.

"No, I won't," she said, shaking her head. "I wouldn't, even before I knew he was your dog."

"Why?"

"Because Miss Prissy is going to have pups."

"Miss Prissy?"

"That's the name of my dog, and she's going to have pups and your dog will be their papa, and I wouldn't want their papa to get shot."

I stared at her again, and again I had to look down. I wanted to thank her, but I didn't know the right words. So I fished around in my pocket and brought out an Indian arrowhead that I'd found the day before and gave that to her.

She took it and stared at it for a little bit, with her eyes shining, then shoved it deep into a long pocket she had sewn to her dress.

"I won't never, never tell," she said, then

whirled and tore out for the house, running as fast as she could.

I went down and sat by the spring awhile. It seemed like I liked Bud Searcy a lot better than I ever had before, even if he did talk too much and spit tobacco juice all over the place. But I was still bothered. If Lisbeth had caught Old Yeller stealing stuff at the settlement, then somebody else might, too. And if they did, they were sure liable to shoot him. A family might put up with one of its own dogs stealing from them if he was a good dog. But for a dog that left home to steal from everybody else—well, I didn't see much chance for him if he ever got caught.

After Bud Searcy had eaten a hearty supper and talked awhile longer, he finally rode off home, with Lisbeth riding behind him. I went then and gathered the eggs and held three back. I called Old Yeller off from the house and broke the eggs on a flat rock, right under his nose and tried to get him to eat them. But he wouldn't. He acted like he'd never heard tell that eggs were fit to eat. All he'd do was stand there and wiggle his tail and try to lick me in the face.

It made me mad. "You thievin' rascal," I said. "I ought to get a club and break your back—in fourteen different places."

But I didn't really mean it, and I didn't say it loud and ugly. I knew that if I did, he'd fall over and start yelling like he was dying. And there I'd be—in a fight with Little Arliss again.

"When they shoot you, I'm going to laugh," I told him.

But I knew that I wouldn't.

SEVEN

I did considerable thinking on what Lisbeth Searcy had told me about Old Yeller and finally went and told Mama.

"Why, that old rogue!" she said. "We'll have to try to figure some way to keep him from prowling. Everybody in the settlement will be mad at us if we don't."

"Somebody'll shoot him," I said.

"Try tying him," she said.

So I tried tying him. But we didn't have any bailing wire in those days, and he could chew through anything else before you could turn your back. I tried him with rope and then with big thick rawhide string that I cut from a cowhide hanging across the top rail of the yard fence. It was the same thing in both cases. By the time we could get off to bed, he'd done chewed them in two and was gone.

"Let's try the corncrib," Mama said on the third night.

Which was a good idea that might have worked if it hadn't been for Little Arliss.

I took Old Yeller out and put him in the corncrib and the second that he heard the door shut on him, he set up a yelling and a howling that brought Little Arliss on the run. Mama and I both tried to explain to him why we needed to shut the dog up, but Little Arliss was too mad to listen. You can't explain things very well to somebody who is screaming his head off and chunking you with rocks as fast as he can pick them up. So that didn't work, either.

"Well, it looks like we're stumped," Mama said.

I thought for a minute and said, "No, Mama. I believe we've got one other chance. That's to shut him up in the same room with me and Little Arliss every night."

"But he'll sleep in the bed with you boys," Mama said, "and the first thing you know, you'll both be scratching fleas and having mange and breaking out with ringworms."

"No, I'll put him a cowhide on the floor and make him sleep there," I said.

So Mama agreed and I spread a cowhide on the floor beside our bed and we shut Old Yeller in and didn't have a bit more trouble.

Of course, Old Yeller didn't sleep on the cowhide. And once, a good while later, I did break out with a little ringworm under my left arm. But I rubbed it with turpentine, just like Mama always did, and it soon went away. And after that, when we fed Old Yeller cornmeal mush or fresh meat, he ate it and did well on it and never one time bothered our chicken nests.

About that time, too, the varmints got to pestering us so much that a lot of times Old Yeller and I were kept busy nearly all night long.

It was the coons, mainly. The corn was ripening into roasting ears now, and the coons would come at night and strip the shucks back with their little hands, and gnaw the milky kernels off the cob. Also, the watermelons were beginning to turn red inside and the skunks would come and open up little round holes in the rinds and reach in with their forefeet and drag out the juicy insides to eat. Sometimes coyotes would come and eat watermelons, too; and now and then a deer would jump into the field and eat corn, melons, and peas.

So Old Yeller and I took to sleeping in the corn patch every night. We slept on the cowhide that Yeller never would sleep on at the house. That is, we did when we got to sleep. Most of the night, we'd be up fighting coons. We slept out in the middle of the patch, where Yeller could scent a coon clear to the fence on every side. We'd lie there on the cowhide and look up at the stars and listen to the warm night breeze rustling the corn blades. Sometimes I'd wonder what the stars were and what kept them hanging up there so high and bright and if Papa, 'way off up yonder in Kansas, could see the same stars I could see.

I was getting mighty lonesome to see Papa. With the help of Old Yeller, I was taking care of things all right; but I was sure beginning to wish that he'd come back home.

Then I'd think awhile about the time when I'd get big enough to go off on a cow drive myself, riding my own horse, and see all the big new country of plains and creeks and rivers and mountains and timber and new towns and Indian camps. Then, finally, just about the time I started drifting off to sleep, I'd hear Old Yeller rise to his feet and go padding off through the corn. A minute later, his yelling bay would lift from some part of the corn patch, and I'd hear the fighting squawl of some coon caught stealing corn. Then I'd jump to my feet and go running through the corn, shouting encouragement to Old Yeller.

"Git him, Yeller," I'd holler. "Tear him up!"

And that's what Old Yeller would be trying to do; but a boar coon isn't an easy thing to tear up. For one thing, he'll fight you from sundown till sunup. He's not big for size, but the longer you fight him, the bigger he seems to get. He fights you with all four feet and every tooth in his head and enough courage for an animal five times his size.

On top of that, he's fighting inside a thick hide that fills a dog's mouth like a wad of loose sacking. The dog has a hard time ever really biting him. He just squirms and twists around inside that hide and won't quit fighting even after the dog's got enough and is ready to throw the fight to him. Plenty of times, Papa and I had seen a boar coon whip

Bell, run him off, then turn on us and chase us clear out of a cornfield.

It was easy for me to go running through the dark cornfields, yelling for Old Yeller to tear up a thieving coon, but it wasn't easy for Old Yeller to do it. He'd be yelling and the coon would be squawling and they'd go wallowing and clawing and threshing through the corn, popping the stalks as they broke them off, making such an uproar in the night that it sounded like murder. But, generally, when the fight was all over, the coon went one way and Old Yeller the other, both of them pretty well satisfied to call it quits.

We didn't get much sleep of a night while all this was going on, but we had us a good time and saved the corn from the coons.

The only real bad part of it was the skunks. What with all the racket we made coon fighting, the skunks didn't come often. But when one did come, we were in a mess.

Old Yeller could handle a skunk easy enough. All he had to do was rush in, grab it by the head and give it a good shaking. That would break the skunk's neck, but it wouldn't end the trouble. Because not even a hoot owl can kill a skunk without getting sprayed with his scent. And skunk scent is a smell that won't quit. After every skunk killing, Old Yeller would get so sick that he could hardly stand it. He'd snort and drool and slobber and vomit. He'd roll and wallow in the dirt and go dragging his body through tall weeds, trying to get the scent off; but he couldn't. Then finally, he'd give up and come lie down on the cowhide with me. And of course he'd smell so bad that I couldn't stand him and have to go off and try to sleep somewhere else. Then he'd follow me and get his feelings hurt because I wouldn't let him sleep with me.

Papa always said that breathing skunk scent was the best way in the world to cure a head cold. But this was summertime, when Old Yeller and I didn't have head colds. We would just as soon that the skunks stayed out of the watermelons and let us alone.

Working there, night after night, guarding our precious bread corn from the varmints, I came to see what I would have been up against if I'd had it to do without the help of Old Yeller. By myself, I'd have been run to death and still probably wouldn't have saved the corn. Also, look at all the fun I would have missed if I'd been alone, and how lonesome I would have been. I had to admit Papa had been right when he'd told me how bad I needed a dog.

I saw that even more clearly when the spotted heifer had her first calf.

Our milk cows were all old-time longhorn cattle and didn't give a lot of milk. It was real hard to find one that would give much more than her calf could take. What we generally had to do was milk five or six cows to get enough milk for just the family.

But we had one crumpled-horn cow named Rose that gave a lot of milk, only she was getting old, and Mama kept hoping that each of her heifer calves would turn out to be as good a milker as Rose. Mama had tried two or three, but none of them proved to be any good. And then along came this spotted one that was just raw-boned and ugly enough to make a good milk cow. She had the bag for it, too, and Mama was certain this time that she'd get a milk cow to replace Rose.

The only trouble was, this heifer Spot, as we called her, had been snaky wild from the day she was born. Try to drive her with the other cattle, and she'd run off and hide. Hem her up in a corner and try to get your hands on her, and she'd turn on you and make fight. Mama had been trying all along to get Spot gentled before she had her first calf, but it was no use. Spot didn't want to be friends with anybody. We knew she was going to give us a pile of trouble when we set out to milk her.

I failed to find Spot with the rest of our milk cows one evening, and when I went to drive them up the next day, she was still gone.

"It's time for her to calve," Mama said, "and I'll bet she's got one."

So the next morning I went further back in the hills and searched all over. I finally came across her, holed up in a dense thicket of bee myrtle close to a little seep spring. I got one brief glimpse of a wobbly, long-legged calf before Spot snorted and took after me. She ran me clear to the top of the next high ridge before she turned back.

I made another try. I got to the edge of the thicket and picked me up some rocks. I went to hollering and chunking into the brush, trying to scare her and the calf out. I got her out, all right, but she wasn't scared. She came straight for me with her horns lowered, bawling her threats as she came. I had to turn tail a second time, and again she chased me clear to the top of that ridge.

I tried it one more time, then went back to the house and got Old Yeller. I didn't know if he knew anything about driving cattle or not, but I was willing to bet that he could keep her from chasing me.

And he did. I went up to the edge of the thicket and started hollering and chunking rocks into it. Here came the heifer, madder than ever, it looked like. I yelled at Old Yeller. "Get her, Yeller," I hollered. And Yeller got her. He pulled the neatest trick I ever saw a dog pull on a cow brute.

Only I didn't see it the first time. I was getting away from there too fast. I'd stumbled and fallen to my knees when I turned to run from Spot's charge, and she was too close behind for me to be looking back and watching what Old Yeller was doing. I just heard the scared bawl she let out and the crashing of the brush as Old Yeller rolled her into it.

I ran a piece further, then looked back. The heifer was scrambling to her feet in a cloud of dust and looking like she didn't know any more about what had happened than I did. Then she caught sight of Old Yeller. She snorted, stuck her tail in the air and made for him. Yeller ran like he was scared to death, then cut back around a thicket. A second later, he was coming in behind Spot.

Without making a sound, he ran up beside her, made his leap and set his teeth in her nose.

I guess it was the weight of him that did it. I saw him do it lots of times later, but never did quite understand how. Anyway, he just set his teeth in her nose, doubled himself up in a tight ball, and swung on. That turned the charging heifer a flip. Her heels went straight up in the air over her head. She landed flat on her back with all four feet sticking up. She hit the ground so hard that it sounded like she ought to bust wide open.

I guess she felt that way about it, too. Anyhow, after taking that second fall, she didn't have much fight left in her. She just scrambled to her feet and went trotting back into the thicket, lowing to her calf.

I followed her, with Old Yeller beside me, and we drove her out and across the hills to the cow lot. Not one time did she turn on us again. She did try to run off a couple of times, but all I had to do was send Old Yeller in to head her. And the second she caught sight of him, she couldn't turn fast enough to get headed back in the right direction.

It was the same when we got her into the cowpen. Her bag was all in a strut with milk that the calf couldn't hold. Mama said we needed to get that milk out. She came with a bucket and I took it, knowing I had me a big kicking fight on my hands if I ever hoped to get any milk.

The kicking fight started. The first time I touched Spot's bag, she reached out with a flying hind foot, aiming to kick my head off and coming close to doing it. Then she wheeled on me and put me on top of the rail fence as quick as a squirrel could have made it.

Mama shook her head. "I was hoping she wouldn't be that way," she said. "I always hate to have to tie up a heifer to break her for milking. But I guess there's no other way with this one."

I thought of all the trouble it would be, having to tie up that Spot heifer, head and feet, twice a day, every day, for maybe a month or more. I looked at Old Yeller, standing just outside the pen.

"Yeller," I said, "you come in here."

Yeller came bounding through the rails.

Mama said: "Why, son, you can't teach a heifer to stand with a dog in the pen. Especially one with a young calf. She'll be fighting at him all the time, thinking he's a wolf or something trying to get her calf."

I laughed. "Maybe it won't work," I said, "but I bet you one thing. She won't be fighting Old Yeller."

She didn't, either. She lowered her horns and rolled her eyes as I brought Old Yeller up to her.

"Now, Yeller," I said, "you stand here and watch her."

Old Yeller seemed to know just what I wanted. He walked right up to where he could almost touch his nose to hers and stood there, wagging his stub tail. And she didn't charge him or run from him. All she did was stand there and sort of tremble. I went back and milked out her strutted bag and she didn't offer to kick me one time, just flinched and drew up a little when I first touched her.

"Well, that does beat all," Mama marveled. "Why, at that rate, we'll have her broke to milk in a week's time."

Mama was right. Within three days after we started, I could drive Spot into the pen, go right up and milk her, and all she'd do was stand there and stare at Old Yeller. By the end of the second week, she was standing and belching and chewing her cud—the gentlest cow I ever milked.

After all that, I guess you can see why I nearly died when a man rode up one day and claimed Old Yeller.

EIGHT

The man's name was Burn Sanderson. He was a young man who rode a good horse and was mighty nice and polite about taking his hat off to Mama when he dismounted in front of our cabin. He told Mama who he was. He said he was a newcomer to Salt Licks. He said that he'd come from down San Antonio way with a little bunch of cattle that he was grazing over in the Devil's River country. He said he couldn't afford to hire riders, so he'd brought along a couple of dogs to help him herd his cattle. One of these dogs, the best one, had disappeared. He'd inquired around about it at Salt Licks, and Bud Searcy had told him that we had the dog.

"A big yeller dog?" Mama asked, looking sober and worried.

"Yessum," the man said, then added with a grin, "and the worse egg sucker and camp robber you ever laid eyes on. Steal you blind, that old devil will; but there was never a better cow dog born."

Mama turned to me. "Son, call Old Yeller," she said.

I stood frozen in my tracks. I was so full of panic that I couldn't move or think.

"Go on, Son," Mama urged. "I think he and Little Arliss must be playing down about the creek somewhere."

"But Mama!" I gasped. "We can't do without Old Yeller. He's—"

"Travis!"

Mama's voice was too sharp. I knew I was whipped. I turned and went toward the creek, so mad at Bud Searcy that I couldn't see straight. Why couldn't he keep his blabber mouth shut?

"Come on up to the house," I told Little Arliss.

I guess the way I said it let him know that something real bad was happening. He didn't argue or stick out his tongue or any-

90

thing. He just got out of the water and followed me back to the house and embarrassed Mama and the young man nearly to death because he came packing his clothes in one hand instead of wearing them.

I guess Burn Sanderson had gotten an idea of how much we thought of Old Yeller, or maybe Mama had told some things about the dog while I was gone to the creek. Anyhow, he acted uncomfortable about taking the dog off. "Now, Mrs. Coates," he said to Mama, "your man is gone, and you and the boys don't have much protection here. Bad as I need that old dog, I can make out without him until your man comes."

But Mama shook her head.

"No, Mr. Sanderson," she said. "He's your dog; and the longer we keep him, the harder it'll be for us to give him up. Take him along. I can make the boys understand."

The man tied his rope around Old Yeller's neck and mounted his horse. That's when Little Arliss caught on to what was happening. He threw a wall-eyed fit. He screamed and he hollered. He grabbed up a bunch of rocks and went to throwing them at Burn Sanderson. One hit Sanderson's horse in the flank. The horse bogged his head and went to pitching and bawling and grunting. This excited Old Yeller. He chased after the horse, baying him at the top of his voice. And what with Mama running after Little Arliss, hollering for him to shut up and quit throwing those rocks, it was altogether the biggest and loudest commotion that had taken place around our cabin for a good long while.

When Burn Sanderson finished riding the pitch out of his scared horse, he hollered at Old Yeller. He told him he'd better hush up that racket before he got his brains beat out. Then he rode back toward us, wearing a wide grin.

His grin got wider as he saw how Mama and I were holding Little Arliss. We each had him by one wrist and were holding him clear off the ground. He couldn't get at any more rocks to throw that way, but it sure didn't keep him from dancing up and down in the air and screaming.

"Turn him loose," Sanderson said with a big laugh. "He's not going to throw any more rocks at me."

He swung down from his saddle. He came and got Little Arliss and loved him up till he hushed screaming. Then he said: "Look, boy, do you really want that thieving old dog?"

He held Little Arliss off and stared him straight in the eyes, waiting for Arliss to answer. Little Arliss stared straight back at him and didn't say a word.

"Well, do you?" he insisted.

Finally, Little Arliss nodded, then tucked his chin and looked away.

"All right," Burn Sanderson said. "We'll make a trade. Just between you and me. I'll let you keep the old rascal, but you've got to do something for me."

He waited till Little Arliss finally got up the nerve to ask what, then went on: "Well, it's like this. I've hung around over there in that cow camp, eating my own cooking till I'm so starved out, I don't hardly throw a shadow. Now, if you could talk your mama into feeding me a real jam-up meal of woman-cooked grub, I think it would be worth at least a one-eared yeller dog. Don't you?"

I didn't wait to hear any more. I ran off. I was so full of relief that I was about to pop. I knew that if I didn't get out of sight in a hurry, this Burn Sanderson was going to catch me crying.

*   *   *

93

Mama cooked the best dinner that day I ever ate. We had roast venison and fried catfish and stewed squirrel and blackeyed peas and cornbread and flour gravy and butter and wild honey and hog-plum jelly and fresh buttermilk. I ate till it seemed like my eyeballs would pop out of my head, and still didn't make anything like the showing that Burn Sanderson made. He was a slim man, not nearly as big as Papa, and I never could figure out where he was putting all that grub. But long before he finally sighed and shook his head at the last of the squirrel stew, I was certain of one thing: he sure wouldn't have any trouble throwing a shadow on the ground for the rest of that day. A good, black shadow.

After dinner, he sat around for a while, talking to me and Mama and making Little Arliss some toy horses out of dried cornstalks. Then he said his thank-yous to Mama and told me to come with him. I followed with him while he led his horse down to the spring for water. I remembered how Papa had led me away from the house like this the day he left and knew by that that Burn Sanderson had something he wanted to talk to me about.

At the spring, he slipped the bits out of

his horse's mouth to let him drink, then turned to me.

"Now, boy," he said, "I didn't want to tell your mama this. I didn't want to worry her. But there's a plague of hydrophobia making the rounds, and I want you to be on the lookout for it."

I felt a scare run through me. I didn't know much about hydrophobia, but after what Bud Searcy had told about his uncle that died, chained to a tree, I knew it was something bad. I stared at Burn Sanderson and didn't say anything.

"And there's no mistake about it," he said. "I've done shot two wolves, a fox, and one skunk that had it. And over at Salt Licks, a woman had to kill a bunch of house cats that her younguns had been playing with. She wasn't sure, but she couldn't afford to take any chances. And you can't, either."

"But how will I know what to shoot and what not to?" I wanted to know.

"Well, you can't hardly tell at first," he said. "Not until they have already gone to foaming at the mouth and are reeling with the blind staggers. Any time you see a critter acting that way, you know for sure. But you watch for others that aren't that far along. You take a pet cat. If he takes to spitting and

95

fighting at you for no reason, you shoot him. Same with a dog. He'll get mad at nothing and want to bite you. Take a fox or a wildcat. You know they'll run from you; when they don't run, and try to make fight at you, shoot 'em. Shoot anything that acts unnatural, and don't fool around about it. It's too late after they've already bitten or scratched you."

Talk like that made my heart jump up in my throat till I could hardly get my breath. I looked down at the ground and went to kicking around some rocks.

"You're not scared, are you, boy? I'm only telling you because I know your papa left you in charge of things. I know you can handle whatever comes up. I'm just telling you to watch close and not let anything—*anything*—get to you or your folks with hydrophobia. Think you can do it?"

I swallowed. "I can do it," I told him. "I'm not scared."

The sternness left Burn Sanderson's face. He put a hand on my shoulder, just as Papa had the day he left.

"Good boy," he said. "That's the way a man talks."

Then he gripped my shoulder real tight, mounted his horse and rode off through the brush. And I was so scared and mixed up about the danger of hydrophobia that it was clear into the next day before I even thought about thanking him for giving us Old Yeller.

NINE

A boy, before he really grows up, is pretty much like a wild animal. He can get the wits scared clear out of him today and by tomorrow have forgotten all about it.

At least, that's the way it was with me. I was plenty scared of the hydrophobia plague that Burn Sanderson told me about. I could hardly sleep that night. I kept picturing in my mind mad dogs and mad wolves reeling about with the blind staggers, drooling slobbers and snapping and biting at everything in sight. Maybe biting Mama and Little Arliss, so that they got the sickness and went mad, too. I lay in bed and shuddered and shivered and dreamed all sorts of nightmare happenings.

Then, the next day, I went to rounding up and marking hogs and forgot all about the plague.

Our hogs ran loose on the range in those days, the same as our cattle. We fenced them out of the fields, but never into a pasture; we had no pastures. We never fed them, unless maybe it was a little corn that we threw to them during a bad spell in the winter. The rest of the time, they rustled for themselves.

They slept out and ate out. In the summertime, they slept in the cool places around the water holes, sometimes in the water. In the winter, they could always tell at least a day ahead of time when a blizzard was on the way; then they'd gang up and pack tons of leaves and dry grass and sticks into some dense thicket or cave. They'd pile all this into a huge bed and sleep on until the cold spell blew over.

They ranged all over the hills and down into the canyons. In season, they fed on acorns, berries, wild plums, prickly-pear apples, grass, weeds, and bulb plants which they rooted out of the ground. They especially liked the wild black persimmons that the Mexicans called *chapotes*.

Sometimes, too, they'd eat a newborn calf if the mama cow couldn't keep them horned away. Or a baby fawn that the doe had left hidden in the tall grass. Once, in a real dry time, Papa and I saw an old sow standing belly deep in a drying up pothole of water, catching and eating perch that were trapped in there and couldn't get away.

Most of these meat eaters were old hogs, however. Starvation, during some bad drought or extra cold winter, had forced them to eat anything they could get hold of. Papa said they generally started out by feeding on the carcass of some deer or cow that had died, then going from there to catching and killing live meat. He told a tale about how one old range hog had caught him when he was a baby and his folks got there just barely in time to save him.

It was that sort of thing, I guess, that always made Mama so afraid of wild hogs. The least little old biting shoat could make her take cover. She didn't like it a bit when I started out to catch and mark all the pigs that our sows had raised that year. She knew we had it to do, else we couldn't tell our hogs from those of the neighbors. But she didn't like the idea of my doing it alone.

"But I'm not working hogs alone, Mama," I pointed out. "I've got Old Yeller, and Burn Sanderson says he's a real good hog dog."

"That doesn't mean a thing," Mama said. "All hog dogs are good ones. A good one is the only kind that can work hogs and live. But the best dog in the world won't keep you from getting cut all to pieces if you ever make a slip."

Well, Mama was right. I'd worked with Papa enough to know that any time you messed with a wild hog, you were asking for trouble. Let him alone, and he'll generally snort and run from you on sight, the same as a deer. But once you corner him, he's the most dangerous animal that ever lived in Texas. Catch a squealing pig out of the bunch, and you've got a battle on your hands. All of them will turn on you at one time and here they'll come, roaring and popping their teeth, cutting high and fast with gleaming white tushes that they keep whetted to the sharpness of knife points. And there's no bluff to them, either. They mean business. They'll kill you if they can get to you; and if you're not fast footed and don't keep a close watch, they'll get to you.

They had to be that way to live in a country where the wolves, bobcats, panther, and bear were always after them, trying for a bait of fresh hog meat. And it was because of this that nearly all hog owners usually left four or five old barrows, or "bar' hogs," as we called them, to run with each bunch of sows. The bar' hogs weren't any more vicious than the boars, but they'd hang with the sows and help them protect the pigs and shoats, when generally the boars pulled off to range alone.

I knew all this about range hogs, and plenty more; yet I still wasn't bothered about the job facing me. In fact, I sort of looked forward to it. Working wild hogs was always exciting and generally proved to be a lot of fun.

I guess the main reason I felt this way was because Papa and I had figured out a quick and nearly foolproof way of doing it. We could catch most of the pigs we needed to mark and castrate without ever getting in reach of the old hogs. It took a good hog dog to pull off the trick; but the way Burn Sanderson talked about Old Yeller, I was willing to bet that he was that good.

He was, too. He caught on right away.

We located our first bunch of hogs at a seep spring at the head of a shallow dry wash that led back toward Birdsong Creek.

There were seven sows, two long-tushed old bar' hogs, and fourteen small shoats.

They'd come there to drink and to wallow around in the potholes of soft cool mud.

They caught wind of us about the same time I saw them. The old hogs threw up their snouts and said "Woo-oof!" Then they all tore out for the hills, running through the rocks and brush almost as swiftly and silently as deer.

"Head 'em, Yeller," I hollered. "Go get 'em boy!"

But it was a waste of words. Old Yeller was done gone.

He streaked down the slant, crossed the draw, and had the tail-end pig caught by the hind leg before the others knew he was after them.

The pig set up a loud squeal. Instantly, all the old hogs wheeled. They came at Old Yeller with their bristles up, roaring and popping their teeth. Yeller held onto his pig until I thought for a second they had him. Then he let go and whirled away, running toward me, but running slow. Slow enough that the old hogs kept chasing him, thinking every second that they were going to catch him the next.

When they finally saw that they couldn't,

the old hogs stopped and formed a tight circle. They faced outward around the ring, their rumps to the center where all the squealing pigs were gathered. That way, they were ready to battle anything that wanted to jump on them. That's the way they were used to fighting bear and panther off from their young, and that's the way they aimed to fight us off.

But we were too smart, Old Yeller and I. We knew better than to try to break into that tight ring of threatening tushes. Anyhow, we didn't need to. All we needed was just to move the hogs along to where we wanted them, and Old Yeller already knew how to do this.

Back he went, right up into their faces, where he pestered them with yelling bays and false rushes till they couldn't stand it. With an angry roar, one of the barrows broke the ring to charge him. Instantly, all the others charged, too.

They were right on Old Yeller again. They were just about to get him. Just let them get a few inches closer, and one of them would slam a four-inch tush into his soft belly.

The thing was, Old Yeller never would let them gain the last few inches on him. They cut and slashed at him from behind and both sides, yet he never was quite there. Always he was just a little bit beyond their reach, yet still so close that they couldn't help thinking that the next try was sure to get him.

It was a blood-chilling game Old Yeller played with the hogs, but one that you could see he enjoyed by the way he went at it. Give him time, and he'd take that bunch of angry hogs clear down out of the hills and into the pens at home if that's where I wanted them —never driving them, just leading them along.

But that's where Papa and I had other hog hunters out-figured. We almost never took our hogs to the pens to work them any more. That took too much time. Also, after we got them penned, there was still the dangerous job of catching the pigs away from the old ones.

I hollered at Old Yeller. "Bring 'em on, Yeller," I said. Then I turned and headed for a big gnarled liveoak tree that stood in a clear patch of ground down the draw apiece.

I'd picked out that tree because it had a huge branch that stuck out to one side. I went and looked the branch over and saw that it was just right. It was low, yet still far enough above the ground to be out of reach of the highest-cutting hog.

I climbed up the tree and squatted on the branch. I unwound my rope from where I'd packed it coiled around my waist and shook out a loop. Then I hollered for Old Yeller to bring the hogs to me.

He did what I told him. He brought the fighting hogs to the tree and rallied them in a ring around it. Then he stood back, holding them there while he cocked his head sideways at me, wanting to know what came next.

I soon showed him. I waited till one of the pigs came trotting under my limb. I dropped my loop around him, gave it a quick yank, and lifted him, squealing and kicking, up out of the shuffling and roaring mass of hogs below. I clamped him between my knees, pulled out my knife, and went to work on him. First I folded his right ear and sliced out a three-cornered gap in the top side, a mark that we called an overbit. Then, from the under side of his left ear, I slashed off a long strip that ran clear to the point. That is what we called an underslope. That had him marked for me. Our mark was overbit the right and underslope the left.

Other settlers had other marks, like crop

the right and underbit the left, or two underbits in the right ear, or an overslope in the left and an overbit in the right. Everybody knew the hog mark of everybody else and we all respected them. We never butchered or sold a hog that didn't belong to us or marked a pig following a sow that didn't wear our mark.

Cutting marks in a pig's ear is bloody work, and the scared pig kicks and squeals like he's dying; but he's not really hurt. What hurts him is the castration, and I never did like that part of the job. But it had to be done, and still does if you want to eat hog meat. Let a boar hog get grown without cutting his seeds out, and his meat is too tough and rank smelling to eat.

The squealing of the pig and the scent of his blood made the hogs beneath me go nearly wild with anger. You never heard such roaring and teeth-popping, as they kept circling the tree and rearing up on its trunk, trying to get to me. The noise they made and the hate and anger that showed in their eyes was enough to chill your blood. Only, I was used to the feeling and didn't let it bother me. That is, not much. Sometimes I'd let my mind slip for a minute and get to thinking how they'd slash me to pieces if I happened to fall out of the tree, and I'd feel a sort of cold shudder run all through me. But Papa had told me right from the start that fear was a right and natural feeling for anybody, and nothing to be ashamed of.

"It's a thing of your mind," he said, "and you can train your mind to handle it just like you can train your arm to throw a rock."

Put that way, it made sense to be afraid; so I hadn't bothered about that. I'd put in all my time trying to train my mind not to let fear stampede me. Sometimes it did yet, of course, but not when I was working hogs. I'd had enough experience at working hogs that now I could generally look down and laugh at them.

I finished with the first pig and dropped it to the ground. Then, one after another, I roped the others, dragged them up into the tree, and worked them over.

A couple of times, the old hogs on the ground got so mad that they broke ranks and charged Old Yeller. But right from the start, Old Yeller had caught onto what I wanted. Every time they chased him from the tree, he'd just run off a little way and circle back, then stand off far enough away that they'd rally around my tree again.

In less than an hour, I was done with the

job, and the only trouble we had was getting the hogs to leave the tree after I was finished. After going to so much trouble to hold the hogs under the tree, Old Yeller had a hard time understanding that I finally wanted them out of the way. And even after I got him to leave, the hogs were so mad and so suspicious that I had to squat there in the tree for nearly an hour longer before they finally drifted away into the brush, making it safe for me to come down.

TEN

With hogs ranging in the woods like that, it was hard to know for certain when you'd found them all. But I kept a piece of ear from every pig I marked. I carried the pieces home in my pockets and stuck them on a sharp-pointed stick which I kept hanging in the corn crib. When the count reached forty-six and I couldn't seem to locate any new bunches of hogs, Mama and I decided that was all the pigs the sows had raised that year. So I had left off hog hunting and started getting ready to gather corn when Bud Searcy paid us another visit. He told me about one bunch of hogs I'd missed.

"They're clear back in that bat cave country, the yonder side of Salt Branch," he said. "Rosal Simpson ran into them a couple of days ago, feeding on pear apples in them prickly-pear flats. Said there was five pigs following three sows wearing your mark. Couple of old bar' hogs ranging with them."

I'd never been that far the other side of Salt Branch before, but Papa told me about the bat cave. I figured I could find the place. So early the next morning, I set out with Old Yeller, glad for the chance to hunt hogs a while longer before starting in on the corn gathering. Also, if I was lucky and found the hogs early, maybe I'd have time left to visit the cave and watch the bats come out.

Papa had told me that was a real sight, the way the bats come out in the late afternoon. I was sure anxious to go see it. I always like to go see the far places and strange sights.

Like one place on Salt Branch that I'd found. There was a high, undercut cliff there and some birds building their nests against the face of it. They were little gray, sharp-winged swallows. They gathered sticky mud out of a hog wallow and carried it up and stuck it to the bare rocks of the cliff, shaping the mud into little bulging nests with a single hole in the center of each one. The young birds hatched out there and stuck their heads out through the holes to get at the worms and bugs the grown birds brought to them. The mud nests were so thick on the face of the cliff that, from a distance, the wall looked like it was covered with honeycomb.

There was another place I liked, too. It was a wild, lonesome place, down in a deep canyon that was bent in the shape of a horseshoe. Tall trees grew down in the canyon and leaned out over a deep hold of clear water. In the trees nested hundreds of long-shanked herons, blue ones and white ones with black wing tips. The herons built huge ragged nests of sticks and trash and sat around in the trees all day long, fussing and staining the tree branches with their white droppings. And beneath them, down in the clear water, yard-long catfish lay on the sandy bottom, waiting to gobble up any young birds that happened to fall out of the nests.

The bat cave sounded like another of those wild places I liked to see. I sure hoped I could locate the hogs in time to pay it a visit while I was close by.

We located the hogs in plenty of time; but before we were done with them, I didn't want to go see a bat cave or anything else.

Old Yeller struck the hogs' trail at a water hole. He ran the scent out into a regular forest of prickly pear. Bright red apples fringed the edges of the pear pads. In places where the hogs had fed, bits of peel and black seeds and red juice stain lay on the ground.

The sight made me wonder again how a hog could be tough enough to eat prickly-pear apples with their millions of little hair-like spines. I ate them, myself, sometimes; for pear apples are good eating. But even after I'd polished them clean by rubbing them in the sand, I generally wound up with several stickers in my mouth. But the hogs didn't seem to mind the stickers. Neither did the wild turkeys or the pack rats or the little big-eared ringtail cats. All of those creatures came to the pear flats when the apples started turning red.

Old Yeller's yelling bay told me that he'd caught up with the hogs. I heard their rumbling roars and ran through the pear clumps toward the sound. They were the hogs that Rosal Simpson had sent word about. There were five pigs, three sows, and a couple of bar' hogs, all but the pigs wearing our mark. Their faces bristled with long pear spines that they'd got stuck with, reaching for apples. Red juice stain was smeared all over their snouts. They stood, backed up against a big prickly-pear clump. Their anger had their bristles standing in high fierce ridges along their backbones. They roared and popped their teeth and dared me or Old Yeller to try to catch one of the squealing pigs.

I looked around for the closest tree. It stood better than a quarter of a mile off. It was going to be rough on Old Yeller, trying to lead them to it. Having to duck and dodge around in those prickly pear, he was bound to come out bristling with more pear spines than the hogs had in their faces. But I couldn't see any other place to take them. I struck off toward the tree, hollering at Old Yeller to bring them along.

A deep cut-bank draw ran through the pear flats between me and the huge mesquite tree I was heading for, and it was down in the bottom of this draw that the hogs balked. They'd found a place where the flood waters had undercut one of the dirt banks to form a shallow cave.

They'd backed up under the bank, with the pigs behind them. No amount of barking and pestering by Old Yeller could get

them out. Now and then, one of the old bar'
hogs would break ranks to make a quick cutting lunge at the dog. But when Yeller
leaped away, the hog wouldn't follow up.
He'd go right back to fill the gap he'd left in
the half circle his mates had formed at the
front of the cave. The hogs knew they'd
found a natural spot for making a fighting
stand, and they didn't aim to leave it.

I went back and stood on the bank above
them, looking down, wondering what to do.
Then it came to me that all I needed to do
was go to work. This dirt bank would serve
as well as a tree. There were the hogs right
under me. They couldn't get to me from
down there, not without first having to go
maybe fifty yards down the draw to find a
place to get out. And Old Yeller wouldn't let
them do that. It wouldn't be easy to reach
beneath that undercut bank and rope a pig,
but I believed it could be done.

I took my rope from around my waist and
shook out a loop. I moved to the lip of the
cut bank. The pigs were too far back under
me for a good throw. Maybe if I lay down on
my stomach, I could reach them.

I did. I reached back under and picked up
the first pig, slick as a whistle. I drew him up
and worked him over. I dropped him back

and watched the old hogs sniff his bloody wounds. Scent of his blood made them madder, and they roared louder.

I lay there and waited. A second pig moved out from the back part of the cave that I couldn't quite see. He still wasn't quite far enough out. I inched forward and leaned further down, to where I could see better. I could reach him with my loop now.

I made my cast, and that's when it happened. The dirt bank broke beneath my weight. A wagon load of sand caved off and spilled down over the angry hogs. I went with the sand.

I guess I screamed. I don't know. It happened too fast. All I can really remember is the wild heart-stopping scare I knew as I tumbled, head over heels, down among those killer hogs.

The crumbling sand all but buried the hogs. I guess that's what saved me, right at the start. I remember bumping into the back of one old bar' hog, then leaping to my feet in a smothering fog of dry dust. I jumped blindly to one side as far as I could. I broke to run, but I was too late. A slashing tush caught me in the calf of my right leg.

A searing pain shot up into my body. I screamed. I stumbled and went down. I screamed louder then, knowing I could never get to my feet in time to escape the rush of angry hogs roaring down upon me.

It was Old Yeller who saved me. Just like he'd saved Little Arliss from the she bear. He came in, roaring with rage. He flung himself between me and the killer hogs. Fangs bared, he met them head on, slashing and snarling. He yelled with pain as the savage tushes ripped into him. He took the awful punishment meant for me, but held his ground. He gave me that one-in-a-hundred chance to get free.

I took it. I leaped to my feet. In wild terror, I ran along the bed of that dry wash, cut right up a sloping bank. Then I took out through the forest of prickly pear. I ran till a forked stick tripped me and I fell.

It seemed like that fall, or maybe it was the long prickly-pear spines that stabbed me in the hip, brought me out of my scare. I sat up, still panting for breath and with the blood hammering in my ears. But I was all right in my mind again. I yanked the spines out of my hip, then pulled up my slashed pants to look at my leg. Sight of so much blood nearly threw me into another panic. It was streaming out of the cut and clear down into my shoe.

I sat and stared at it for a moment and shivered. Then I got hold of myself again. I wiped away the blood. The gash was a bad one, clear to the bone, I could tell, and plenty long. But it didn't hurt much; not yet, that is. The main hurting would start later, I guessed, after the bleeding stopped and my leg started to get stiff. I guessed I'd better hurry and tie up the place and get home as quick as I could. Once that leg started getting stiff, I might not make it.

I took my knife and cut a strip off the tail of my shirt. I bound my leg as tight as I could. I got up to see if I could walk with the leg wrapped as tight as I had it, and I could.

But when I set out, it wasn't in the direction of home. It was back along the trail through the prickly pear.

I don't quite know what made me do it. I didn't think to myself: "Old Yeller saved my life and I can't go off and leave him. He's bound to be dead, but it would look mighty shabby to go home without finding out for sure. I have to go back, even if my hurt leg gives out on me before I can get home."

I didn't think anything like that. I just started walking in that direction and kept walking till I found him.

He lay in the dry wash, about where I'd

119

left it to go running through the prickly pear. He'd tried to follow me, but was too hurt to keep going. He was holed up under a broad slab of red sandstone rock that had slipped off a high bank and now lay propped up against a round boulder in such a way as to form a sort of cave. He'd taken refuge there from the hogs. The hogs were gone now, but I could see their tracks in the sand around the rocks, where they'd tried to get at him from behind. I'd have missed him, hidden there under that rock slab, if he hadn't whined as I walked past.

I knelt beside him and coaxed him out from under the rocks. He grunted and groaned as he dragged himself toward me. He sank back to the ground, his blood-smeared body trembling while he wiggled his stub tail and tried to lick my hog-cut leg.

A big lump came up into my throat. Tears stung my eyes, blinding me. Here he was, trying to lick my wound, when he was bleeding from a dozen worse ones. And worst of all was his belly. It was ripped wide open and some of his insides were bulging out through the slit.

It was a horrible sight. It was so horrible that for a second I couldn't look at it. I wanted to run off. I didn't want to stay and look at something that filled me with such a numbing terror.

But I didn't run off. I shut my eyes and made myself run a hand over Old Yeller's head. The stickiness of the blood on it made my flesh crawl, but I made myself do it. Maybe I couldn't do him any good, but I wasn't going to run off and leave him to die, all by himself.

Then it came to me that he wasn't dead yet and maybe he didn't have to die. Maybe there was something that I could do to save him. Maybe if I hurried home, I could get Mama to come back and help me. Mama'd know what to do. Mama always knew what to do when somebody got hurt.

I wiped the tears from my eyes with my shirt sleeves and made myself think what to do. I took off my shirt and tore it into strips. I used a sleeve to wipe the sand from the belly wound. Carefully, I eased his entrails back into place. Then I pulled the lips of the wound together and wound strips of my shirt around Yeller's body. I wound them tight and tied the strips together so they couldn't work loose.

All the time I worked with him, Old Yeller didn't let out a whimper. But when I shoved him back under the rock where he'd be out of the hot sun, he started whining. I guess he knew that I was fixing to leave him, and he wanted to go, too. He started crawling back out of his hole.

I stood and studied for a while. I needed something to stop up the opening so Yeller couldn't get out. It would have to be something too big and heavy for him to shove aside. I thought of a rock and went looking for one. What I found was even better. It was an uprooted and dead mesquite tree, lying on the back of the wash.

The stump end of the dead mesquite was big and heavy. It was almost too much for me to drag in the loose sand. I heaved and sweated and started my leg to bleeding again. But I managed to get that tree stump where I wanted it.

I slid Old Yeller back under the rock slab. I scolded him and made him stay there till I could haul the tree stump into place.

Like I'd figured, the stump just about filled the opening. Maybe a strong dog could have squeezed through the narrow opening that was left, but I didn't figure Old Yeller could. I figured he'd be safe in there till I could get back.

Yeller lay back under the rock slab now, staring at me with a look in his eyes that made that choking lump come into my throat again. It was a begging look, and Old Yeller wasn't the kind to beg.

I reached in and let him lick my hand. "Yeller," I said, "I'll be back. I'm promising that I'll be back."

Then I lit out for home in a limping run. His howl followed me. It was the most mournful howl I ever heard.

ELEVEN

It looked like I'd never get back to where I'd left Old Yeller. To begin with, by the time I got home, I'd traveled too far and too fast. I was so hot and weak and played out that I was trembling all over. And that hog-cut leg was sure acting up. My leg hadn't gotten stiff like I'd figured. I'd used it too much. But I'd strained the cut muscle. It was jerking and twitching long before I got home; and after I got there, it wouldn't stop.

That threw a big scare into Mama. I argued and fussed, trying to tell her what a bad shape Old Yeller was in and how we needed to hurry back to him. But she wouldn't pay me any mind.

She told me: "We're not going anywhere until we've cleaned up and doctored that leg. I've seen hog cuts before. Neglect them, and they can be as dangerous as snakebite. Now, you just hold still till I get through."

I saw that it wasn't any use, so I held still while she got hot water and washed out the cut. But when she poured turpentine into the place, I couldn't hold still. I jumped and hollered and screamed. It was like she'd bur'nt me with a red-hot iron. It hurt worse than when the hog slashed me. I hollered with hurt till Little Arliss turned up and went to crying, too. But when the pain finally left my leg, the muscle had quit jerking.

Mama got some clean white rags and bound up the place. Then she said, "Now, you lie down on that bed and rest. I don't want to see you take another step on that leg for a week."

I was so stunned that I couldn't say a word. All I could do was stare at her. Old Yeller, lying 'way off out there in the hills, about to die if he didn't get help, and Mama telling me I couldn't walk.

I got up off the stool I'd been sitting on. I said to her, "Mama, I'm going back after Old

Yeller. I promised him I'd come back, and that's what I aim to do." Then I walked through the door and out to the lot.

By the time I got Jumper caught, Mama had her bonnet on. She was ready to go, too. She looked a little flustered, like she didn't know what to do with me, but all she said was, "How'll we bring him back?"

"On Jumper," I said. "I'll ride Jumper and hold Old Yeller in my arms."

"You know better than that," she said. "He's too big and heavy. I might lift him up to you, but you can't stand to hold him in your arms that long. You'll give out."

"I'll hold him," I said. "If I give out, I'll rest. Then we'll go on again."

Mama stood tapping her foot for a minute while she gazed off across the hills. She said, like she was talking to herself, "We can't use the cart. There aren't any roads, and the country is too rough."

Suddenly she turned to me and smiled. "I know what. Get that cowhide off the fence. I'll go get some pillows."

"Cowhide?"

"Tie it across Jumper's back," she said. "I'll show you later."

I didn't know what she had in mind, but it didn't much matter. She was going with me.

127

I got the cowhide and slung it across Jumper's back. It rattled and spooked him so that he snorted and jumped from under it.

"You Jumper!" I shouted at him. "You hold still."

He held still the next time. Mama brought the pillows and a long coil of rope. She had me tie the cowhide to Jumper's back and bind the pillows down on top of it. Then she lifted Little Arliss up and set him down on top of the pillows.

"You ride behind him," she said to me. "I'll walk."

We could see the buzzards gathering long before we got there. We could see them wheeling black against the blue sky and dropping lower and lower with each circling. One we saw didn't waste time to circle. He came hurtling down at a long-slanted dive, his ugly head outstretched, his wings all but shut against his body. He shot past, right over our heads, and the *whooshing* sound his body made in splitting the air sent cold chills running all through me. I guessed it was all over for Old Yeller.

Mama was walking ahead of Jumper. She looked back at me. The look in her eyes told me that she figured the same thing. I got so sick that it seemed like I couldn't stand it.

But when we moved down into the prickly-pear flats, my misery eased some. For suddenly, up out of a wash ahead rose a flurry of flapping wings. Something had disturbed those buzzards and I thought I knew what it was.

A second later, I was sure it was Old Yeller. His yelling bark sounded thin and weak, yet just to hear it made me want to holler and run and laugh. He was still alive. He was still able to fight back!

The frightened buzzards had settled back to the ground by the time we got there. When they caught sight of us, though, they got excited and went to trying to get off the ground again. For birds that can sail around in the air all day with hardly more than a movement of their wing tips, they sure were clumsy and awkward about getting started. Some had to keep hopping along the wash for fifty yards, beating the air with their huge wings, before they could finally take off. And then they were slow to rise. I could have shot a dozen of them before they got away if I'd thought to bring my gun along.

There was a sort of crazy light shining in Old Yeller's eyes when I looked in at him. When I reached to drag the stump away, he snarled and lunged at me with bared fangs.

I jerked my hands away just in time and shouted "Yeller!" at him. Then he knew I wasn't a buzzard. The crazy light went out of his eyes. He sank back into the hole with a loud groan like he'd just had a big load taken off his mind.

Mama helped me drag the stump away. Then we reached in and rolled his hurt body over on its back and slid him out into the light.

Without bothering to examine the blood-caked cuts that she could see all over his head and shoulders, Mama started unwinding the strips of cloth from around his body.

Then Little Arliss came crowding past me, asking in a scared voice what was the matter with Yeller.

Mama stopped. "Arliss," she said, "do you think you could go back down this sandy wash here and catch Mama a pretty green-striped lizard? I thought I saw one down there around that first bend."

Little Arliss was as pleased as I was surprised. Always before, Mama had just sort of put up with his lizard-catching. Now she was wanting him to catch one just for her. A de-lighted grin spread over his face. He turned and ran down the wash as hard as he could.

Mama smiled up at me, and suddenly I understood. She was just getting Little Arliss out of the way so he wouldn't have to look at the terrible sight of Yeller's slitted belly.

She said to me: "Go jerk a long hair out of Jumper's tail, Son. But stand to one side, so he won't kick you."

I went and stood to one side of Jumper and jerked a long hair out of his tail. Sure enough, he snorted and kicked at me, but he missed. I took the hair back to Mama, wondering as much about it as I had about the green-striped lizard. But when Mama pulled a long sewing needle from her dress front and poked the small end of the tail hair through the eye, I knew then.

"Horse hair is always better than thread for sewing up a wound," she said. She didn't say why, and I never did think to ask her.

Mama asked me if any of Yeller's entrails had been cut and I told her that I didn't think so.

"Well, I won't bother them then," she said. "Anyway, if they are, I don't think I could fix them."

It was a long, slow job, sewing up Old Yeller's belly. And the way his flesh would flinch and quiver when Mama poked the needle through, it must have hurt. But if it

131

did, Old Yeller didn't say anything about it. He just lay there and licked my hands while I held him.

We were wrapping him up in some clean rags that Mama had brought along when here came Little Arliss. He was running as hard as he'd been when he left. He was grinning and hollering at Mama. And in his right hand he carried a green-striped lizard, too.

How on earth he'd managed to catch anything as fast running as one of those green-striped lizards, I don't know; but he sure had one.

You never saw such a proud look as he wore on his face when he handed the lizard to Mama. And I don't guess I ever saw a more helpless look on Mama's face as she took it. Mama had always been squeamish about lizards and snakes and bugs and things, and you could tell that it just made her flesh crawl to have to touch this one. But she took it and admired it and thanked Arliss. Then she asked him if he'd keep it for her till we got home. Which Little Arliss was glad to do.

"Now, Arliss," she told him, "we're going to play a game. We're playing like Old Yeller is sick and you are taking care of him. We're going to let you both ride on a cowhide, like the sick Indians do sometimes."

It always pleased Little Arliss to play any sort of game, and this was a new one that he'd never heard about before. He was so anxious to get started that we could hardly keep him out from underfoot till Mama could get things ready.

As soon as she took the cowhide off Jumper's back and spread it hair-side down upon the ground, I began to get the idea. She placed the soft pillows on top of the hide, then helped me to ease Old Yeller's hurt body onto the pillows.

"Now, Arliss," Mama said, "you sit there on the pillows with Old Yeller and help hold him on. But remember now, don't play with him or get on top of him. We're playing like he's sick, and when your dog is sick, you have to be real careful with him."

It was a fine game, and Little Arliss fell right in with it. He sat where Mama told him to. He held Old Yeller's head in his lap, waiting for the ride to start.

It didn't take long. I'd already tied a rope around Jumper's neck, leaving the loop big enough that it would pull back against his shoulders. Then, on each side of Jumper, we tied another rope into the one knotted about his shoulders, and carried the ends of them back to the cowhide. I took my knife and cut two slits into the edge of the cowhide, then tied a rope into each one. We measured to get each rope the same length and made sure they were far enough back that the cowhide wouldn't touch Jumper's heels. Like most mules, Jumper was mighty fussy about anything touching his heels.

"Now, Travis, you ride him," Mama said, "and I'll lead him."

"You better let me walk," I argued. "Jumper's liable to throw a fit with that hide rattling along behind him, and you might not can hold him by yourself."

"You ride him," Mama said. "I don't want you walking on that leg any more. If Jumper acts up one time, I'll take a club to him!"

We started off, with Little Arliss crowing at what a fine ride he was getting on the dragging hide. Sure enough, at the first sound of that rattling hide, old Jumper acted up. He snorted and tried to lunge to one side. But Mama yanked down on his bridle and said, "Jumper, you wretch!" I whacked him between the ears with a dead stick. With the two of us coming at him like that, it was more than Jumper wanted. He

settled down and went to traveling as quiet
as he generally pulled a plow, with just now
and then bending his neck around to take a
look at what he was dragging. You could tell
he didn't like it, but I guess he figured he'd
best put up with it.

Little Arliss never had a finer time than
he did on that ride home. He enjoyed every
long hour of it. And a part of the time, I
don't guess it was too rough on Old Yeller.
The cowhide dragged smooth and even as
long as we stayed in the sandy wash. When
we left the wash and took out across the
flats, it still didn't look bad. Mama led
Jumper in a long roundabout way, keeping
as much as she could to the openings where
the tall grass grew. The grass would bend
down before the hide, making a soft cushion
over which the hide slipped easily. But this
was a rough country, and try as hard as she
could, Mama couldn't always dodge the
rocky places. The hide slid over the rocks,
the same as over the grass and sand, but it
couldn't do it without jolting the riders
pretty much.

Little Arliss would laugh when the hide
raked along over the rocks and jolted him
till his teeth rattled. He got as much fun out

of that as the rest of the ride. But the jolting hurt Old Yeller till sometimes he couldn't hold back his whinings.

When Yeller's whimperings told us he was hurting too bad, we'd have to stop and wait for him to rest up. At other times, we stopped to give him water. Once we got water out of a little spring that trickled down through the rocks. The next time was at Birdsong Creek.

Mama'd pack water to him in my hat. He was too weak to get up and drink; so Mama would hold the water right under his nose and I'd lift him up off the pillows and hold him close enough that he could reach down and lap the water up with his tongue.

Having to travel so far and so slow and with so many halts, it looked like we'd never get him home. But we finally made it just about the time it got dark enough for the stars to show.

By then, my hurt leg was plenty stiff, stiff and numb. It was all swelled up and felt as dead as a chunk of wood. When I slid down off Jumper's back, it wouldn't hold me. I fell clear to the ground and lay in the dirt, too tired and hurt to get up.

Mama made a big to-do about how weak

and hurt I was, but I didn't mind. We'd gone and brought Old Yeller home, and he was still alive. There by the starlight, I could see him licking Little Arliss's face.

Little Arliss was sound asleep.

TWELVE

For the next couple of weeks, Old Yeller and I had a rough time of it. I lay on the bed inside the cabin and Yeller lay on the cowhide in the dog run, and we both hurt so bad that we were wallowing and groaning and whimpering all the time. Sometimes I hurt so bad that I didn't quite know what was happening. I'd hear grunts and groans and couldn't tell if they were mine or Yeller's. My leg had swelled up till it was about the size of a butter churn. I had such a wild hot fever that Mama nearly ran herself to death, packing fresh cold water from the spring, which she used to bathe me all over, trying to run my fever down.

When she wasn't packing water, she was out digging prickly-pear roots and hammering them to mush in a sack, then binding the mush to my leg for a poultice.

We had lots of prickly pear growing close to the house, but they were the big tall ones and their roots were no good. The kind that make a good poultice are the smaller size. They don't have much top, but lots of knotty roots, shaped sort of like sweet potatoes. That kind didn't grow close to the house. Along at the last, Mama had to go clear over to the Salt Licks to locate that kind.

When Mama wasn't waiting on me, she was taking care of Old Yeller. She waited on him just like she did me. She was getting up all hours of the night to doctor our wounds, bathe us in cold water, and feed us when she could get us to eat. On top of that, there were the cows to milk, Little Arliss to look after, clothes to wash, wood to cut, and old Jumper to worry with.

The bad drought that Bud Searcy predicted had come. The green grass all dried up till Jumper was no longer satisfied to eat it. He took to jumping the field fence and eating the corn that I'd never yet gotten around to gathering.

Mama couldn't let that go on; that was our bread corn. Without it, we'd have no bread for the winter. But it looked like for a while that there wasn't any way to save it. Mama would go to the field and run Jumper out; then before she got her back turned good, he'd jump back in and go to eating corn again.

Finally, Mama figured out a way to keep Jumper from jumping. She tied a drag to him. She got a rope and tied one end of it to his right forefoot. To the other end, she tied a big heavy chunk of wood. By pulling hard, Jumper could move his drag along enough to graze and get to water; but any time he tried to rear up for a jump, the drag held him down.

The drag on Jumper's foot saved the corn but it didn't save Mama from a lot of work. Jumper was always getting his chunk of wood hung up behind a bush or rock, so that he couldn't get away. Then he'd have himself a big scare and rear up, fighting the rope and falling down and pitching and bawling. If Mama didn't hear him right away, he'd start braying, and he'd keep it up till she went and loosened the drag.

Altogether, Mama sure had her hands full, and Little Arliss wasn't any help. He was too little to do any work. And with neither of us to play with, he got lonesome. He'd follow Mama around every step she made, getting in the way and feeling hurt because she didn't have time to pay him any mind. When he wasn't pestering her, he was pestering me. A dozen times a day, he'd come in to stare at me and say: "Whatcha doin' in bed, Travis? Why doncha get up? Why doncha get up and come play with me?"

He nearly drove me crazy till the day Bud Searcy and Lisbeth came, bringing the pup.

I didn't know about the pup at first. I didn't even know that Lisbeth had come. I heard Bud Searcy's talk to Mama when they rode up, but I was hurting too bad even to roll over and look out the door. I remember just lying there, being mad at Searcy for coming. I knew what a bother he'd be to Mama. For all his talk of looking after the women and children of Salt Licks while the men were gone, I knew he'd never turn a hand to any real work. You wouldn't catch him offering to chop wood or gather in a corn crop. All he'd do was sit out under the dog run all day, talking and chewing tobacco and spitting juice all over the place. On top of that, he'd expect Mama to cook him up a good dinner and maybe a supper if he took a notion to stay that long. And Mama had ten times too much to do, like it was.

In a little bit, though, I heard a quiet step at the door. I looked up. It was Lisbeth. She stood with her hands behind her back, staring at me with her big solemn eyes.

"You hurting pretty bad?" she asked.

I was hurting a-plenty, but I wasn't admitting it to a girl. "I'm doing all right," I said.

"We didn't know you'd got hog cut, or we'd have come sooner," she said.

I didn't know what to say to that, so I didn't say anything.

"Well, anyhow," she said, "I brung you a surprise."

I was too sick and worn out to care about a surprise right then; but there was such an eager look in her eyes that I knew I had to say "What?" or hurt her feelings, so I said "What?"

"One of Miss Prissy's pups!" she said.

She brought her hands around from behind her back. In the right one, she held a dog pup about a big as a year-old possum. It was a dirty white in color and speckled all over with blue spots about the size of cow ticks. She held it by the slack hide at the back of its neck. It hung there, half asleep, sagging in its own loose hide like it was dead.

"Born in a badger hole," she said. "Seven of them. I brung you the best one!"

I thought: If that puny-looking thing is the best one, Miss Prissy must have had a sorry litter of pups. But I didn't say so. I said: "He sure looks like a dandy."

"He is," Lisbeth said. "See how I've been holding him, all this time, and he hasn't said a word."

I'd heard that one all my life—that if a pup didn't holler when you held him up by the slack hide of his neck, he was sure to turn out to be a gritty one. I didn't think much of that sign. Papa always put more stock in what color was inside a pup's mouth. If the pup's mouth was black inside, Papa said that was the one to chose. And that's the way I felt about it.

But right now I didn't care if the pup's mouth was pea-green on the inside. All I wanted was just to quit hurting.

I said, "I guess Little Arliss will like it," then knew I'd said the wrong thing. I could tell by the look in her eyes that I'd hurt her feelings, after all.

She didn't say anything. She just got real still and quiet and kept staring at me till I couldn't stand it and had to look away. Then she turned and went out of the cabin and gave the pup to Little Arliss.

It made me mad, her looking at me like that. What did she expect, anyhow? Here I was laid up with a bad hog cut, hurting so bad I could hardly get my breath, and her expecting me to make a big to-do over a little old puny speckled pup.

I had me a dog. Old Yeller was all cut up, worse than I was, but he was getting well. Mama had told me that. So what use did I have for a pup? Be all right for Little Arliss to play with. Keep him occupied and out from underfoot. But when Old Yeller and I got well and took to the woods again, we wouldn't have time to wait around on a fool pup, too little to follow.

I lay there in bed, mad and fretful all day, thinking how silly it was for Lisbeth to expect me to want a pup when I already had me a full-grown dog. I lay there, just waiting for a chance to tell her so, too; only she never did come back to give me a chance. She stayed outside and played with Little Arliss and the pup till her grandpa finally wound up his talking and tobacco spitting and got ready to leave. Then I saw her and Little Arliss come past the door, heading for where I could hear her grandpa saddling his horse. She looked in at me, then looked away, and suddenly I wasn't mad at her any more. I felt sort of mean. I wished now I could think of the right thing to say about the pup, so I could call her back and tell her. I didn't want her to go off home with her feelings still hurt.

But before I could think of anything, I heard her grandpa say to Mama: "Now Mrs. Coates, you all are in a sort of bind here, with your man gone and that boy crippled up. I been setting out here all evening, worrying about it. That's my responsibility, you know, seeing that everybody's taken care of while the men are gone, and I think now I've got a way figured. I'll just leave our girl Lisbeth here to help you all out."

Mama said in a surprised voice: "Why, Mr. Searcy, there's no need for that. It's mighty kind of you and all, but we'll make out all right."

"No, now, Mrs. Coates; you got too big a load to carry, all by yourself. My Lisbeth, she'll be proud to help out."

"But," Mama argued, "she's such a little girl, Mr. Searcy. She's probably never stayed away from home of a night."

"She's little," Bud Searcy said, "but she's stout and willing. She's like me; when folks are in trouble, she'll pitch right in and do her part. You just keep her here now. You'll see what a big help she'll be."

Mama tried to argue some more, but Bud Searcy wouldn't listen. He just told Lisbeth to be a good girl and help Mama out, like she was used to helping out at home. Then he mounted and rode on off.

THIRTEEN

I was like Mama. I didn't think Lisbeth
Searcy would be any help around the
place. She was too little and too skinny. I figured she'd just be an extra bother for
Mama.

But we were wrong. Just like Bud Searcy
said, she was a big help. She could tote water
from the spring. She could feed the
chickens, pack in wood, cook cornbread,
wash dishes, wash Little Arliss, and sometimes even change the prickly-pear poultice
on my leg.

She didn't have to be told, either. She was
right there on hand all the time, just looking

for something to do. She was a lot better about that than I ever was. She wasn't as big and she couldn't do as much as I could, but she was more willing.

She didn't even back off when Mama hooked Jumper to the cart and headed for the field to gather in the corn. That was a job I always hated. It was hot work, and the corn shucks made my skin itch and sting till sometimes I'd wake up at night scratching like I'd stumbled into a patch of bull nettles.

But it didn't seem to bother Lisbeth. In fact, it looked like she and Mama and Little Arliss had a real good time gathering corn. I'd see them drive past the cabin, all three of them sitting on top of a cartload of corn. They would be laughing and talking and having such a romping big time, playing with the speckled pup, that before long I half wished I was able to gather corn too.

In a way, it sort of hurt my pride for a little old girl like Lisbeth to come in and take over my jobs. Papa had left me to look after things. But now I was laid up, and here was a girl handling my work about as good as I could. Still, she couldn't get out and mark hogs or kill meat or swing a chopping axe....

Before they were finished gathering corn,

however, we were faced with a trouble a whole lot too big for any of us to handle.

The first hint of it came when the Spot heifer failed to show up one evening at milking time. Mama had come in too late from the corn gathering to go look for her before dark, and the next morning she didn't need to. Spot came up, by herself; or rather, she came past the house.

I heard her first. The swelling in my leg was about gone down. I was weak as a rain-chilled chicken, but most of the hurting had stopped. I was able to sit up in bed a lot and take notice of things.

I heard a cow coming toward the house. She was bawling like cows do when they've lost a calf or when their bags are stretched too tight with milk. I recognized Spot's voice.

Spot's calf recognized it, too. It had stood hungry in the pen all night and now it was nearly crazy for a bait of milk. I could hear it blatting and racing around in the cowpen, so starved it could hardly wait.

I called to Mama. "Mama," I said, "you better go let old Spot in to her calf. I hear her coming."

"That pesky Spot," I heard her say impatiently. "I don't know what's got into her, staying out all night like that and letting her calf go hungry."

I heard Mama calling to Spot as she went out to the cowpen. A little later, I heard Spot beller like a fighting bull, then Mama's voice rising high and sharp. Then here came Mama, running into the cabin, calling for Lisbeth to hurry and bring in Little Arliss. There was scare in Mama's voice. I sat up in bed as Lisbeth came running in, dragging Little Arliss after her.

Mama slammed the door shut, then turned to me. "Spot made fight at me," she said. "I can't understand it. It was like I was some varmint that she'd never seen before."

Mama turned and opened the door a crack. She looked out, then threw the door wide open and stood staring toward the cowpen.

"Why, look at her now," she said. "She's not paying one bit of attention to her calf. She's just going on past the cowpen like her calf wasn't there. She's acting as crazy as if she'd got hold of a bait of pea vine."

There was a little pea vine that grew wild all over the hills during wet winters and bloomed pale lavender in the spring. Cattle and horses could eat it, mixed with grass, and get fat on it. But sometimes when they got too big a bait of it alone, it poisoned them. Generally, they'd stumble around with the blind staggers for a while, then gradually get well. Sometimes, though, the pea vine killed them.

I sat there for a moment, listening to Spot. She was bawling again, like when I first heard her. But now she was heading off into the brush again, leaving her calf to starve. I wondered where she'd gotten enough pea vine to hurt her.

"But Mama," I said, "she couldn't have eaten pea vine. The pea vine is all dead and gone this time of year."

Mama turned and looked at me, then looked away. "I know," she said. "That's what's got me so worried."

I thought of what Burn Sanderson had told me about animals that didn't act right. I said, "Cows don't ever get hydrophobia, do they?"

I saw Lisbeth start at the word. She stared at me with big solemn eyes.

"I don't know," Mama said. "I've seen dogs with it, but I've never heard of a cow brute having it. I just don't know."

In the next few days, while Old Yeller and I healed fast, we all worried and watched.

All day and all night, Spot kept right on

doing what she did from the start: she walked and she bawled. She walked mostly in a wide circle that brought her pretty close to the house about twice a day and then carried her so far out into the hills that we could just barely hear her. She walked with her head down. She walked slower and her bawling got weaker as she got weaker; but she never stopped walking and bawling.

When the bull came, he was worse, and a lot more dangerous. He came two or three days later. I was sitting out under the dog run at the time. I'd hobbled out to sit in a chair beside Old Yeller, where I could scratch him under his chewed-off ear. That's where he liked to be scratched best. Mama was in the kitchen, cooking dinner. Lisbeth and Little Arliss had gone off to the creek below the spring to play with the pup and to fish for catfish. I could see them running and laughing along the bank, chasing after grasshoppers for bait.

Then I heard this moaning sound and turned to watch a bull come out of the brush. He was the roan bull, the one that the droopy-horned *chongo* had dumped into the Mexican cart the day of the fight. But he didn't walk like any bull I'd ever seen before. He walked with his head hung

154

low and wobbling. He reeled and staggered like he couldn't see where he was going. He walked head on into a mesquite tree like it wasn't there, and fell to his knees when he hit it. He scrambled to his feet and came on, grunting and staggering and moaning, heading toward the spring.

Right then, for the first time since we'd brought him home, Old Yeller came up off his cowhide bed. He'd been lying there beside me, paying no attention to sight or sound of the bull. Then, I guess the wind must have shifted and brought him the bull's scent; and evidently that scent told him for certain what I was only beginning to suspect.

He rose, with a savage growl. He moved out toward the bull, so trembly weak that he could hardly stand. His loose lips were lifted in an ugly snarl, baring his white fangs. His hackles stood up in a ragged ridge along the back of his neck and shoulders.

Watching him, I felt a prickling at the back of my own neck. I'd seen him act like that before, but only when there was the greatest danger. Never while just facing a bull.

Suddenly, I knew that Mama and I had been fooling ourselves. Up till now, we'd been putting off facing up to facts. We'd kept hoping that the heifer Spot would get over whatever was wrong with her. Mama and Lisbeth had kept Spot's calf from starving by letting it suck another cow. They'd had to tie the cow's hind legs together to keep her from kicking the calf off; but they'd kept it alive, hoping Spot would get well and come back to it.

Now, I knew that Spot wouldn't get well, and this bull wouldn't, either. I knew they were both deathly sick with hydrophobia. Old Yeller had scented that sickness in this bull and somehow sensed how fearfully dangerous it was.

I thought of Lisbeth and Little Arliss down past the spring. I came up out of my chair, calling for Mama. "Mama!" I said. "Bring me my gun, Mama!"

Mama came hurrying to the door. "What is it, Travis?" she wanted to know.

"That bull!" I said, pointing. "He's mad with hydrophobia and he's heading straight for Lisbeth and Little Arliss."

Mama took one look, said "Oh, my Lord!" in almost a whisper. She didn't wait to get me my gun or anything else. She just tore out for the creek, hollering for Lisbeth and Little Arliss to run, to climb a tree, to do anything to get away from the bull.

I called after her, telling her to wait, to

give me a chance to shoot the bull. I don't guess she ever heard me. But the bull heard her. He tried to turn on her, stumbled and went to his knees. Then he was back on his feet again as Mama went flying past. He charged straight for her. He'd have gotten her, too, only the sickness had his legs too wobbly. This time, when he fell, he rooted his nose into the ground and just lay there, moaning, too weak even to try to get up again.

By this time, Old Yeller was there, baying the bull, keeping out of his reach, but ready to eat him alive if he ever came to his feet again.

I didn't wait to see more. I went and got my gun. I hobbled down to where I couldn't miss and shot the roan bull between the eyes.

FOURTEEN

We couldn't leave the dead bull to lie there that close to the cabin. In a few days, the scent of rotting flesh would drive us out. Also, the carcass lay too close to the spring. Mama was afraid it would foul up our drinking water.

"We'll have to try to drag it further from the cabin and burn it," she said.

"Burn it?" I said in surprise. "Why can't we just leave it for the buzzards and varmints to clean up?"

"Because that might spread the sickness," Mama said. "If the varmints eat it, they might get the sickness too."

Mama went to put the harness on Jumper. I sent Lisbeth to bring me a rope. I doubled the rope and tied it in a loop around the bull's horns. Mama brought Jumper, who snorted and shied away at the sight of the dead animal. Jumper had smelled deer blood plenty of times, so I guess it was the size of the bull that scared him. Or maybe like Yeller, Jumper could scent the dead bull's sickness. I had to talk mean and threaten him with a club before we could get him close enough for Mama to hook the singletree over the loop of rope I'd tied around the bull's horns.

Then the weight of the bull was too much for him. Jumper couldn't drag it. He leaned into his collar and dug in with his hoofs. He grunted and strained. He pulled till I saw the big muscles of his haunches flatten and start quivering. But the best he could do was slide the bull carcass along the ground for about a foot before he gave up.

I knew he wasn't throwing off. Jumper was full of a lot of pesky, aggravating mule tricks; but when you called on him to move a load, he'd move it or bust something.

I called on him again. I drove him at a different angle from the load, hoping he'd have better luck. He didn't. He threw everything he had into the collar, and all he did was pop a link out of his right trace chain. The flying link whistled past my ear with the speed of a bullet. It would have killed me just as dead if it had hit me.

Well, that was it. There was no moving the dead bull now. We could patch up that broken trace for pulling an ordinary load. But it would never be strong enough to pull this one. Even if Jumper was.

I looked at Mama. She shook her head. "I guess there's nothing we can do but burn it here," she said. "But it's going to take a sight of wood gathering."

It did, too. We'd lived there long enough to use up all the dead wood close to the cabin. Now, Mama and Lisbeth had to go 'way out into the brush for it. I got a piece of rawhide string and patched up the trace chain, and Mama and Lisbeth used Jumper to drag up big dead logs. I helped them pile the logs on top of the bull. We piled them up till we had the carcass completely covered, then set fire to them.

In a little bit, the fire was roaring. Sheets of hot flame shot high into the air. The heat and the stench of burnt hair and scorching hide drove us back.

It was the biggest fire I'd ever seen. I

thought there was fire enough there to burn three bulls. But when it began to die down a couple of hours later, the bull carcass wasn't half burnt up. Mama and Lisbeth went back to dragging up more wood.

It took two days and nights to burn up that bull. We worked all day long each day, with Mama and Lisbeth dragging up the wood and me feeding the stinking fire. Then at night, we could hardly sleep. This was because of the howling and snarling and fighting of the wolves lured to the place by the scent of the roasting meat. The wolves didn't get any of it; they were too afraid of the hot fire. But that didn't keep them from gathering for miles around and making the nights hideous with their howlings and snarlings.

And all night long, both nights, Old Yeller crippled back and forth between the fire and the cabin, baying savagely, warning the wolves to keep away.

Both nights, I lay there, watching the eyes of the shifting wolves glow like live mesquite coals in the firelight, and listening to the weak moaning bawl of old Spot still traveling in a circle. I lay there, feeling shivery with a fearful dread that brought up pictures in my mind of Bud Searcy's uncle.

I sure did wish Papa would come home.

As soon as the job of burning the bull was over, Mama told us we had to do the same for the Spot heifer. That was all Mama said about it, but I could tell by the look in her eyes how much she hated to give up. She'd had great hopes for Spot's making us a real milk cow, especially after Old Yeller had gentled her so fast; but that was all gone now.

Mama looked tired, and more worried than I think I'd ever seen her. I guess she couldn't help thinking what I was thinking —that if hydrophobia had sickened one of our cows, it just might get them all.

"I'll do the shooting," I told her. "But I'm going to follow her out a ways from the house to do it. Closer to some wood."

"How about your leg?" Mama asked.

"That leg's getting all right," I told her. "Think it'll do it some good to be walked on."

"Well, try to kill her on bare ground," Mama cautioned. "As dry as it is now, we'll be running a risk of setting the woods afire if there's much old grass around the place."

I waited till Spot circled past the cabin again, then took my gun and followed her, keeping a safe distance behind.

By now, Spot was so sick and starved I could hardly stand to look at her. She didn't look like a cow; she looked more like the skeleton of one. She was just skin and bones. She was so weak that she stumbled as she walked. Half a dozen times she went to her knees and each time I'd think she'd taken her last step. But she'd always get up and go on again—and keep bawling.

I kept waiting for her to cross a bare patch of ground where it would be safe to build a fire. She didn't; and I couldn't drive her, of course. She was too crazy mad to be driven anywhere. I was afraid to mess with her. She might be like the bull. If I ever let her know I was anywhere about, she might go on the fight.

I guess she was a mile from the cabin before I saw that she was about to cross a dry sandy wash, something like the one where Yeller and I had got mixed up with the hogs. That would be a good place, I knew. It was pretty far for us to have to come to burn her, but there was plenty of dry wood around. And if I could drop her out there in that wide sandy wash, there'd be no danger of a fire getting away from us.

I hurried around and got ahead of her. I hid behind a turkey-pear bush on the far side of the wash. But as sick and blind as she was, I think I could have stood out in the broad open without her ever seeing me. I waited till she came stumbling across the sandy bed of the wash, then fired, dropping her in the middle of it.

I'd used up more of my strength than I knew, following Spot so far from the cabin. By the time I got back I was dead beat. The sweat was pouring off me and I was trembling all over.

Mama took one look at me and told me to get to bed. "We'll go start the burning," she said. "You stay on that leg any longer, and it'll start swelling again."

I didn't argue. I knew I was too weak and tired to take another walk that far without rest. So I told Mama where to find Spot and told her to leave Little Arliss with me, and watched her and Lisbeth head out, both mounted on Jumper. Mama was carrying a panful of live coals to start the fire with.

At the last minute, Yeller got up off his cowhide. He stood watching them a minute, like he was trying to make up his mind about something; then he went trotting after them. He was still thin and rough looking and crippling pretty badly in one leg. But I figured he knew better than I did whether or not he was able to travel. I didn't call him back.

As it turned out, it's a good thing I didn't. Only, afterward, I wished a thousand times that I could have had some way of looking ahead to what was going to happen. Then I would have done everything I could to keep all of them from going.

With Little Arliss to look after, I sure didn't mean to drop off to sleep. But I did and slept till sundown, when suddenly I jerked awake, feeing guilty about leaving him. alone so long.

I needn't have worried. Little Arliss was right out there in the yard, playing with the speckled pup. They had themselves a game going. Arliss was racing around the cabin, dragging a short piece of frayed rope. The pup was chasing the rope. Now and then he'd get close enough to pounce on it. Then he'd let out a growl and set teeth into it and try to shake it and hang on at the same time. Generally, he got jerked off his feet and turned a couple of somersets, but that didn't seem to bother him. The next time Arliss came racing past, the pup would tie into the rope again.

I wondered if he wouldn't get some of his baby teeth jerked out at such rough play, but guessed it wouldn't matter. He'd soon be shedding them, anyhow.

I wondered, too, what was keeping Mama and Lisbeth so long. Then I thought how far it was to where the dead cow lay and how long it would take for just the two of them to drag up enough wood and get a fire started, and figured they'd be lucky if they got back before dark.

I went off to the spring after a bucket of fresh water and wondered when Papa would come back. Mama had said a couple of days ago that it was about that time, and I hoped so. For one thing, I could hardly wait to see what sort of horse Papa was going to bring me. But mainly, this hydrophobia plague had me scared. I'd handled things pretty well until that came along. Of course, I'd gotten a pretty bad hog cut, but that could have happened to anybody, even a grown man. And I was about to get well of that. But if the sickness got more of our cattle, I wouldn't know what to do.

FIFTEEN

It wasn't until dark came that I really began to get uneasy about Mama and Lisbeth. Then I could hardly stand it because they hadn't come home. I knew in my own mind why they hadn't: it had been late when they'd started out; they'd had a good long piece to go; and even with wood handy, it took considerable time to drag up enough for the size fire they needed.

And I couldn't think of any real danger to them. They weren't far enough away from the cabin to be lost. And if they were, Jumper knew the way home. Also, Jumper was gentle; there wasn't much chance that he'd scare and throw them off. On top of all that, they had Old Yeller along. Old Yeller might be pretty weak and crippled yet, but he'd protect them from just about anything that might come their way.

Still, I was uneasy. I couldn't help having the feeling that something was wrong. I'd have gone to see about them if it hadn't been for Little Arliss. It was past his suppertime; he was getting hungry and sleepy and fussy.

I took him and the speckled pup inside the kitchen and lit a candle. I settled them on the floor and gave them each a bowl of sweet milk into which I'd crumbled cold cornbread. In a little bit, both were eating out of the same bowl. Little Arliss knew better than that and I ought to have paddled him for doing it. But I didn't. I didn't say a word; I was too worried.

I'd just about made up my mind to put Little Arliss and the pup to bed and go look for Mama and Lisbeth when I heard a sound that took me to the door in a hurry. It was the sound of dogs fighting. The sound came from 'way out there in the dark; but the minute I stepped outside, I could tell that the fight was moving toward the cabin. Also, I recognized the voice of Old Yeller.

It was the sort of raging yell he let out when he was in a fight to the finish. It was the same savage roaring and snarling and squawling that he'd done the day he fought the killer hogs off me.

The sound of it chilled my blood. I stood, rooted to the ground, trying to think what it could be, what I ought to do.

Then I heard Jumper snorting keenly and Mama calling in a frightened voice. "Travis! Travis! Make a light, Son, and get your gun. And hurry!"

I came alive then. I hollered back at her, to let her know that I'd heard. I ran back into the cabin and got my gun. I couldn't think at first what would make the sort of light I needed, then recollected a clump of bear grass that Mama'd recently grubbed out, where she wanted to start a new fall garden. Bear grass has an oily sap that makes it burn bright and fierce for a long time. A pile of it burning would make a big light.

I ran and snatched up four bunches of the half-dried bear grass. The sharp ends of the stiff blades stabbed and stung my arms and chest as I grabbed them up. But I had no time to bother about that. I ran and dumped the bunches in a pile on the bare ground outside the yard fence, then hurried to bring a live coal from the fireplace to start them burning.

I fanned fast with my hat. The bear-grass blades started smoking, giving off their foul smell. A little flame started, flickered and wavered for a moment, then bloomed suddenly and leaped high with a roar.

I jumped back, gun held ready, and caught my first glimpse of the screaming, howling battle that came wheeling into the circle of light. It was Old Yeller, all right, tangled with some animal as big and savage as he was.

Mama called from outside the light's rim. "Careful, Son. And take close aim; it's a big loafer wolf, gone mad."

My heart nearly quit on me. There weren't many of the gray loafer wolves in our part of the country, but I knew about them. They were big and savage enough to hamstring a horse or drag down a full-grown cow. And here was Old Yeller, weak and crippled, trying to fight a mad one!

I brought up my gun, then held fire while I hollered at Mama. "Y'all get in the cabin," I yelled. "I'm scared to shoot till I know you're out of the line of fire!"

I heard Mama whacking Jumper with a

stick to make him go. I heard Jumper snort and the clatter of his hoofs as he went galloping in a wide circle to come up behind the cabin. But even after Mama called from the door behind me, I still couldn't fire. Not without taking a chance on killing Old Yeller.

I waited, my nerves on edge, while Old Yeller and the big wolf fought there in the firelight, whirling and leaping and snarling and slashing, their bared fangs gleaming white, their eyes burning green in the half light.

Then they went down in a tumbling roll that stopped with the big wolf on top, his huge jaws shut tight on Yeller's throat. That was my chance, and one that I'd better make good. As weak as Old Yeller was, he'd never break that throat hold.

There in the wavering light, I couldn't get a true bead on the wolf. I couldn't see my sights well enough. All I could do was guess-aim and hope for a hit.

I squeezed the trigger. The gunstock slammed back against my shoulder, and such a long streak of fire spouted from the gun barrel that it blinded me for a second; I couldn't see a thing.

Then I realized that all the growling and

snarling had hushed. A second later, I was running toward the two still gray forms lying side by side.

For a second, I just knew that I'd killed Old Yeller, too. Then, about the time I bent over him, he heaved a big sort of sigh and struggled up to start licking my hands and wagging that stub tail.

I was so relieved that it seemed like all the strength went out of me. I slumped to the ground and was sitting there, shivering, when Mama came and sat down beside me.

She put one arm across my shoulders and held it there while she told me what had happened.

Like I'd figured, it had taken her and Lisbeth till dark to get the wood dragged up and the fire to going around the dead cow. Then they'd mounted old Jumper and headed for home. They'd been without water all this time and were thirsty. When they came to the crossing on Birdsong Creek, they'd dismounted to get a drink. And while they were lying down, drinking, the wolf came.

He was right on them before they knew it. Mama happened to look up and see the dark hulk of him come bounding toward them across a little clearing. He was snarling as he came, and Mama just barely had time to come to her feet and grab up a dead chinaberry pole before he sprang. She whacked him hard across the head, knocking him to the ground. Then Old Yeller was there, tying into him.

Mama and Lisbeth got back on Jumper and tore out for the house. Right after them came the wolf, like he had his mind fixed on catching them, and nothing else. But old Yeller fought him too hard and too fast. Yeller wasn't big and strong enough to stop him, but he kept him slowed down and fought away from Jumper and Mama and Lisbeth.

"He had to've been mad, son," Mama wound up. "You know that no wolf in his right senses would have acted that way. Not even a big loafer wolf."

"Yessum," I said, "and it's sure a good thing that Old Yeller was along to keep him fought off." I shuddered at the thought of what could have happened without Old Yeller.

Mama waited a little bit, then said in a quiet voice: "It was a good thing for us, Son; but it wasn't good for Old Yeller."

The way she said that gave me a cold feeling in the pit of my stomach. I sat up straighter. "What do you mean?" I said. "Old Yeller's all right. He's maybe chewed up some, but he can't be bad hurt. See, he's done trotting off toward the house."

Then it hit me what Mama was getting at. All my insides froze. I couldn't get my breath.

I jumped to my feet, wild with hurt and scare. "But Mama!" I cried out. "Old Yeller's just saved your life! He's saved my life. He's saved Little Arliss's life! We can't—"

Mama got up and put her arm across my shoulders again. "I know, Son," she said. "But he's been bitten by a mad wolf."

I started off into the blackness of the night while my mind wheeled and darted this way and that, like a scared rat trying to find its way out of a trap.

"But Mama," I said. "We don't know for certain. We could wait and see. We could tie him or shut him up in the corncrib or some place till we know for sure!"

Mama broke down and went to crying then. She put her head on my shoulder and held me so tight that she nearly choked off my breath.

"We can't take a chance, Son," she sobbed. "It would be you or me or Little Arliss or Lisbeth next. I'll shoot him if you can't, but

176

either way, we've got it to do. We just can't take the chance!"

It came clear to me then that Mama was right. We couldn't take the risk. And from everything I had heard, I knew that there was very little chance of Old Yeller's escaping the sickness. It was going to kill something inside me to do it, but I knew then that I had to shoot my big yeller dog.

Once I knew for sure I had it to do, I don't think I really felt anything. I was just numb all over, like a dead man walking.

Quickly, I left Mama and went to stand in the light of the burning bear grass. I reloaded my gun and called Old Yeller back from the house. I stuck the muzzle of the gun against his head and pulled the trigger.

SIXTEEN

Days went by, and I couldn't seem to get over it. I couldn't eat. I couldn't sleep. I couldn't cry. I was all empty inside, but hurting. Hurting worse than I'd ever hurt in my life. Hurting with a sickness there didn't seem to be any cure for. Thinking every minute of my big yeller dog, how we'd worked together and romped together, how he'd fought the she bear off Little Arliss, how he'd saved me from the killer hogs, how he'd fought the mad wolf off Mama and Lisbeth. Thinking that after all this, I'd had to shoot him the same as I'd done the roan bull and the Spot heifer.

Mama tried to talk to me about it, and I let her. But while everything she said made sense, it didn't do a thing to that dead feeling I had.

Lisbeth talked to me. She didn't say much; she was too shy. But she pointed out that I had another dog, the speckled pup.

"He's part Old Yeller," she said. "And he was the best one of the bunch."

But that didn't help any either. The speckled pup might be part Old Yeller, but he wasn't Old Yeller. He hadn't saved all our lives and then been shot down like he was nothing.

Then one night it clouded up and rained till daylight. That seemed to wash away the hydrophobia plague. At least, pretty soon afterward, it died out completely.

But we didn't know that then. What seemed important to us about the rain was that the next morning after it fell, Papa came riding home through the mud.

The long ride to Kansas and back had Papa drawn down till he was as thin and knotty as a fence rail. But he had money in his pockets, a big shouting laugh for everybody, and a saddle horse for me.

The horse was a cat-stepping blue roan with a black mane and tail. Papa put me on him the first thing and made me gallop him in the clearing around the house. The roan had all the pride and fire any grown man would want in his best horse, yet was as gentle as a pet.

"Now, isn't he a dandy?" Papa asked.

I said "Yessir!" and knew that Papa was right and that I ought to be proud and thankful. But I wasn't. I didn't feel one way or another about the horse.

Papa saw something was wrong. I saw him look a question at Mama and saw Mama shake her head. Then late that evening, just before supper, he called me off down to the spring, where we sat and he talked.

"Your mama told me about the dog," he said.

I said "Yessir," but didn't add anything.

"That was rough," he said. "That was as rough a thing as I ever heard tell of happening to a boy. And I'm mighty proud to learn how my boy stood up to it. You couldn't ask any more of a grown man."

He stopped for a minute. He picked up some little pebbles and thumped them into the water, scattering a bunch of hairy-legged water bugs. The bugs darted across the water in all directions.

"Now the thing to do," he went on, "is to

try to forget it and go on being a man."

"How?" I asked. "How can you forget a thing like that?"

He studied me for a moment, then shook his head. "I guess I don't quite mean that," he said. "It's not a thing you can forget. I don't guess it's a thing that you ought to forget. What I mean is, things like that happen. They may seem mighty cruel and unfair, but that's how life is a part of the time.

"But that isn't the only way life is. A part of the time, it's mighty good. And a man can't afford to waste all the good part, worrying about the bad parts. That makes it all bad. . . . You understand?"

"Yessir," I said. And I did understand. Only, it still didn't do me any good. I still felt just as dead and empty.

That went on for a week or better, I guess, before a thing happened that brought me alive again.

It was right at dinnertime. Papa had sent me out to the lot to feed Jumper and the horses. I'd just started back when I heard a commotion in the house. I heard Mama's voice lifted high and sharp. "Why, you thieving little whelp!" she cried out. Then I heard a shrieking yelp, and out the kitchen door came the speckled pup with a big chunk of cornbread clutched in his mouth. He raced around the house, running with his tail clamped. He was yelling and squawling like somebody was beating him to death. But that still didn't keep him from hanging onto that piece of cornbread that he'd stolen from Mama.

Inside the house, I heard Little Arliss. He was fighting and screaming his head off at Mama for hitting his dog. And above it all, I could hear Papa's roaring laughter.

Right then, I began to feel better. Sight of that little old pup, tearing out for the brush with that piece of cornbread seemed to loosen something inside me.

I felt better all day. I went back and rode my horse and enjoyed it. I rode 'way off out in the brush, not going anywhere especially, just riding and looking and beginning to feel proud of owning a real horse of my own.

Then along about sundown, I rode down into Birdsong Creek, headed for the house. Up at the spring, I heard a splashing and hollering. I looked ahead. Sure enough, it was Little Arliss. He was stripped naked and romping in our drinking water again. And right in there, romping with him, was that bread-stealing speckled pup.

I started to holler at them. I started to say:

"*Arliss!* You get that nasty old pup out of our drinking water."

Then I didn't. Instead, I went to laughing. I sat there and laughed till I cried. When all the time I knew that I ought to go beat them to a frazzle for messing up our drinking water.

When finally I couldn't laugh and cry another bit, I rode on up to the lot and turned my horse in. Tomorrow, I thought, I'll take Arliss and that pup out for a squirrel hunt. The pup was still mighty little. But the way I figured it, if he was big enough to act like Old Yeller, he was big enough to start learning to earn his keep.

Old Yeller's Wildlife

(Almost) everything you wanted to know about the animals of the Texas hill country

Longhorn Cattle

Spanish explorers brought long-horned cattle with them, first to the West Indies, then to Mexico. From Mexico the long-horns spread to Texas, where they were raised for beef in the 1800s. Although hardy, longhorns don't grow as fast as other kinds of cattle, which made them less popular with ranchers of the 1900s.

185

Bobcat

Bobcats, named for their short, or bobbed, tails, have adapted well to people. As farms and towns have moved into their territory, they have added chickens and house pets to their normal diet of rabbits and rodents. Their brown fur matches their surroundings — lighter brown in desert areas and darker brown in wooded areas.

Black Bear

At one time you could find black bears in almost any woods of North America. Now they are much scarcer. Black bears measure about five feet long and weigh between 200 and 500 pounds. Their diet includes fruits, berries, insects, and bird eggs.

186

Bobwhite

A member of the quail family, the bobwhite whistles its name. It lives in large family groups called *coveys*. Bobwhites can fly but prefer the ground, where they feed on seeds and insects and build their nests.

Blue Catfish

How many different kinds of catfish are there? More than 2,000! All have two to four pairs of "whiskers," which give them their catlike appearance. Blue catfish have sharp spines on their back and side fins. A cut from a spine can be poisonous, like a bee sting. Blue catfish feed on the bottoms of rivers and ponds.

Javelina

Cousins of the wild hog, javelinas live in the south-western United States, traveling in herds of up to several hundred animals. They rest in the heat of the day, coming out at night to search for fruit, berries, or roots.

Texas Gray Wolf

In the Texas hills it was called the "loafer wolf." But the gray or timber wolf once ranged across most of the United States. Today, its numbers and its territory have been greatly reduced. Gray wolves are tireless hunters who outrun their prey. Working as a team, a wolf pack can bring down a large moose or an elk.

188

Mountain Lion

Early settlers called it a panther or catamount. Its more common name is mountain lion. Once found throughout the forests of the United States, mountain lions now live chiefly in wilderness areas of the West. Night hunters, they commonly prey on deer and elk, and may be eight feet long, tail included.

White-tailed Deer

A white-tailed deer has a tan coat that turns gray in the winter. The underside of its tail is white. When a deer is afraid, it raises its tail, showing a white "flag" that sends a signal to other deer that danger is near.

A Letter from the Texas Hill Country,

1879

A young woman writes to her friend.

My Husband, Col. [Colonel] Day, is building a fence around his pasture, which when done will contain 40,000 acres of land. It is a beautiful country, rolling prairie, covered with good grass, interspersed with timber, through which are beautiful little streams of running water and cool springs.

We have a good stone house with four rooms and a front porch, a smoke house full of hams, breakfast bacon, flour, meal, dried apples, beans, golden and maple syrup by the barrel, splendid pickles, canned corn, tomatoes, grapes, blackberries, strawberries, sugar, coffee, and catsup. I believe that is all we have to eat except cheese and maple sugar, which I keep in my room for my own

Mason, Texas, 1876 A town of the Texas hill country, where Mrs. Day's letter originated, Mason was later the birthplace of Fred Gipson, author of *Old Yeller*.

use. Col. Day shipped his provisions from Austin, one of the nearest railroad points. We get a nice mutton or goat every once in a while or a hind quarter of beef. Then the boys bring in a deer occasionally and every evening some quail or a turkey — we have plenty of wild game.

I have but one neighbor, Mrs. Gatlin, who lives seven miles from me. She spent the day with me day before yesterday. She is a splendid woman; has lived here but two years. I wish you could see her house. It is made of poles stuck straight up and down and covered with boards. That is a paradise compared to the other houses in this country, most of which are dug outs. All of these people who live here are good hearted, but wholly uneducated. Col. Day got me a guitar to bring with me instead of a piano, and they call it a music box and think it very large. What would they think, could they see a piano?

I have but one neighbor, Mrs. Gatlin, who lives seven miles from me.

There are deer, antelope, a few panthers, plenty of snakes, centipedes, tarantulas, wolves, prairie dogs, and polecats out here; so, you see, if I get up a music class out here, they will have to be my pupils.

Col. Day and I are going to Coleman City tomorrow, which is thirty miles north of the ranch; so I stayed home today to write my letters. Here comes a wagon. Who can it be? Well, what do you think! Old Mr. Creswell, the only man for forty miles who has a garden, and he has a good one, has brought over twenty-five watermellons, a sack of string beans, and some nice fresh tomatoes, with his compliments to the "Old Boss" and his boys. Ha, ha, he forgot me, but that is all O.K. I'll just quit my letter a moment and try one of those mellons all the same.

Can't you

visit? Let

me hear

from you.

I'll have to send those mellons to the boys. They camp where they are at work, as it is so far to come home. It is eleven miles from the house to the far side of the pasture.

Do you wonder I weigh 145 pounds? I wish you were here with me. I'll venture you'll never complain again. What do you say, Myrt? Come out and ranch it a while. I'd dance on my head to see you coming. Come to Fort Worth on the cars, then stage to Brownwood, and I'll meet you there with our 'traveling she-bang.' Col. Day got it in St. Louis. It is nice, cost $373, has three seats in it. They can be let down and a bed fixed in it like a sleeping car. We can cook and eat in it, if the weather is raining.

Can't you visit? Let me hear from you, if you will allow me to still be your friend, and I'll promise to do better in the future. Address me at Trap Post Office, Rich Coffee, Texas. It is a little town at the Trap Crossing on the ranch.

1879

COWBOYS
and Cattle Ranching

Yesterday and Today
by Patricia Lauber

The trail boss and cowboys with perhaps three thousand longhorns, the wrangler with 120 horses, the cook with his chuck wagon — that was the outfit that set out in the early spring on a trip north that would take from two to four months. For the first few days the cowboys pressed the cattle hard, covering twenty to twenty-five miles a day. The cattle were as wild as buffaloes and difficult to handle. The cowboys forced the pace in order to trail-break the herd, to hurry it away from the home range, and to tire the cattle so that they would lie down at night.

By the end of the first few days the herd had organized itself into a traveling unit. There was always a natural leader, usually a steer, who took his place at the head of the herd and kept it day after day. Behind him, strung out in a line that might be as much as two miles long, came the rest of the herd, winding across the plains like a many-colored ribbon. The stronger, rangier cattle were in the lead, with the weak or lazy ones bringing up the rear.

The men, like the cattle, had their places. The most able and experienced cowboys rode point, the position at the head of the herd. Their job was to keep the herd on course, to avoid mix-ups with other herds on the trail, and if the cattle were startled, to try to keep stampedes from starting. Other cowboys, known as swing riders and flank riders, traveled beside the cattle. At the end were the dragmen, or drag riders, whose days were spent "eating dust" and urging the stragglers along.

The trail boss saw to everything. He circled the herd. He rode ahead to lay out the

trail if it was new, to find water, and to choose campsites
and bedding grounds for the cattle.

With the home range left well behind, the trail boss
planned to cover ten to fifteen miles a day. By the time the
first light streaked the sky, the cook had the fire going and
breakfast ready and was shouting,
"Roll out! Come an' get it!"
The men ate quickly, saddled
up, and got the herd strung
out and grazing. They let it
graze for two or three miles
before starting to drive
it steadily along. If
possible, there was a
stop for water
around noon.

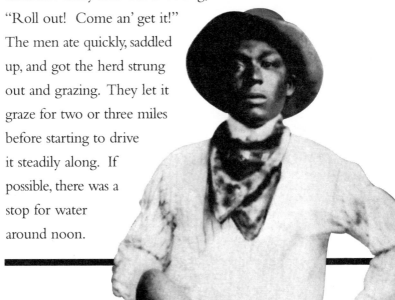

The men ate,
changed horses, and
started the cattle mov-
ing again.

At sundown the
herd was thrown off the
trail to graze. Later the
cowboys drove it onto the
bedding ground and rode
around it in slowly tightening
circles. Forced in together,
the herd lay down.

By then the cook had set up
camp, got the fire going, and had
supper on. The men ate, sitting cross-
legged on the ground, and if they were not too tired, passed
the time by talking, telling jokes, or singing songs of the trail.

Otherwise, they rolled into
their blankets and went to
sleep, except for those who
were riding night watch
on the herd.

The watch changed at 10 P.M., midnight, and 2 A.M., but the routine was always the same. The men rode slowly around the bedded-down cattle, and most sang or hummed as they rode. The rhythms of the songs were slow, matching the steps of the night horses, and the tunes were mournful. Some cowboys sang hymns. Some sang of their work:

Oh say little dogies when are you goin' to lay down
And quit this forever shiftin' around?
My horse is leg-weary and I'm awful tired.
But if you get away I'm sure to get fired.

The cowboys believed that their songs soothed the cattle and kept sudden noises from startling them into a stampede. But the cowboy sang for himself as well in the loneliness of this night watch on the vast and open plains.

Around midnight the cattle stirred, got to their feet, and then lay down in a different position. The night watch went on, ending with breakfast at daybreak. Horses were saddled and then the cattle were started north for another day on the trail.